*Grand
Timber
Lodge*

The Three Rules of the Matadors

Every student at Matador Villa must first learn the three basic rules of the Matadors...

THE FIRST RULE: Students must b̶ ̶ ̶ ̶pared for attack at any time.

THE SECOND RULE: ̶ ̶ ̶ ̶ ̶ ̶ ̶ ̶ ̶ ̶ t all times.

THE THIRD ̶ ̶ ̶ ̶ ̶ ̶ in a fight involving death.

Ace Science Fiction books by Steve Perry

THE MAN WHO NEVER MISSED
MATADORA
THE MACHIAVELLI INTERFACE
coming in July 1986

MATADORA

STEVE PERRY

ACE SCIENCE FICTION BOOKS
NEW YORK

This book is an Ace Science Fiction original edition,
and has never been previously published.

MATADORA

An Ace Science Fiction Book/published by arrangement with
the author

PRINTING HISTORY
Ace Science Fiction edition/February 1986

ISBN: 0-441-52207-6

Ace Science Fiction Books are published by
The Berkley Publishing Group,
200 Madison Avenue, New York, New York 10016.
PRINTED IN THE UNITED STATES OF AMERICA

ACKNOWLEDGMENTS

There are people who helped, directly or otherwise.

Some of those who contributed I can list, and in so doing, offer my thanks: Dianne, Meg, Dal, Stephani, Toni, Carol, Roger, Carol, Slick, Brynne, Beth, Shawna, Sharon, Ginjer, Candy, Vonda, John, Gin, Ray, Jean and, of course, the beautiful Mallory.

They helped. Thanks.

For Dianne, for Dianne!
For Sharon, for all the work;
And for Mary Ann Brown,
Who read my very first
fumbling try.

MATADORA

Part One

"Step by step, walk the thousand mile road."
Miyamoto Musashi

*"Therefore it is necessary to learn how not to be good,
and to use this knowledge and not use it, according to
the necessity of the cause."*
Machiavelli

ONE ⸻

DEATH CAME FOR her from behind a child's game.

There was only a single man this time, but Dirisha saw he was trained by the way he moved, solidly within his own Center. She didn't know him, but she knew what he was: a ronin, like herself. He was a player and it was the Musashi Flex which drove him. He might have seen her work, or maybe heard from somebody who had. So now, he had to test her. It was always the way of it, that testing.

Damn.

Somebody might die, she knew, and death only had two contestants from which to choose. It was no field of honor on which Dirisha Zuri stood, watching her would-be assassin, only a dimly-lit arcade, bounded by banks of holo-proj games and sturz-booths. The place was deserted, save for Dirisha and her stalker—she had chosen it for that

reason. He moved well, this big man with tea-colored skin
and blond hair, but he was all too visible a tail to somebody
with Dirisha's own training.

She nodded at him, resigned. "Armed?"

He shook his head. "Let's do it bare."

"All right." If he were any good, he'd be carrying half
a dozen weapons. He could have a buzzer, buckle blade,
slap-caps, maybe even a projectile pen; Dirisha had those.
His hands were open and empty now, but that didn't mean
anything. If it went against him, he might go for a helper;
certainly she would. Honor was in surviving, not fair play.
But first, you had to know . . .

Tea-skin slid his left foot forward a few centimeters and
turned his body slightly. He brought his hands up, left high,
right low, and stiffened his fingers, curling his thumbs down.
He was four meters away.

Dirisha stood relaxed in a neutral stance and watched
Tea-skin calmly as she tried to figure out his style. One of
the striking systems, obviously, and likely he was a mono-
stylist, too. He could be very good at it, but he gave away
more than he should by his stance; a really experienced
ronin would hide as much as possible until the last moment.

Tea-skin scooted forward half a meter, using the eco-
nomical push-slide of a martial boxer. Karate or kung fu,
Dirisha figured, or one of the myriad variants. He would
be a power-fighter, judging from the swellings of his muscles. He would likely hit hard and depend upon his strength
to carry the fight. All right. She knew she shouldn't expect
anything, that she should simply trance-react to whatever
came, but her experiences wouldn't go away. If she was
right, she might be able to handle him easier, maybe get
away without killing or maiming him.

He moved half a meter closer, sliding across the grimy
tile floor. A blue light from some holoproj game program
strobed across his face and he blinked against it. The same

blue light glinted from her own black skin.

He's nervous, Dirisha thought. A bad sign. For herself, Dirisha felt no fear. She was deeply trained in four Arts, less well-instructed in a handful of others. She would win or lose, that was all. She would essay to perform her techniques correctly, no more, no less; the consequences of failure didn't enter into it. A woman did what a woman had to, the best way she knew how. To do more was impossible, to do less, unthinkable.

Tea-skin slid yet closer, almost within his range and still outside of Dirisha's zone. For a moment, she took time to wonder about the man facing her. What would he be thinking? What he could see was simple enough; a big woman of about thirty, with chocolate skin and green eyes, dressed in a red body suit and tunic, standing loosely and watching. He couldn't know what she had done, where she had been, what forces had formed her into what she was. No, all he could see was another player, a follower of the ancient warrior Musashi, a seeker after martial perfection. A personal test for himself. A bloody battle.

For a brief moment, Dirisha thought about turning and running from the arcade. It seemed pointless to fight this man, pointless to play the game she'd first learned a decade ago on Mti. She wanted the perfection, but this part of it had grown old. She had long since learned to avoid fights when she could, especially with the untrained. At first, the competition had been exciting, it had made her blood sing. Even when she lost and had to spend days or weeks nursing her body back to optimum, it had been a part she'd willingly played, a role she wanted. But now? Now she wished only to learn and be left alone. She avoided other players when she saw them, never issued challenges, kept a low profile at each new dojo. The only thing was, other players knew of her; and, those who did not, would see evidence of her skills in the most simple of movements. She might as well be wearing a flashing sign for those with the same kinds of abilities.

The sound of a breath too sharply indrawn roused Dirisha from her wandering thoughts. Tea-skin was almost ready for his attack. Outwardly, Dirisha gave no sign she noticed; inwardly, she reached for the autotrance—

Tea-skin lunged and drove his fist at Dirisha's throat. It was a deathblow, aimed at crushing her windpipe.

Dirisha pivoted to her right, planted her feet solidly, and grabbed the outstretched arm as she twisted. She applied Atemi Waza Second, a kind of tug-and-loop with her hands, and Tea-skin lost his balance and tumbled forward. If he didn't know how to recover from the fall—the man tucked his shoulder and rolled, coming up in a half-turn so that he faced Dirisha when he regained his feet. It was a move which saved him from a bad fall, but from his attack and recovery, Dirisha knew the more important thing: his skills were no match for hers; the fight was as good as over.

"What say we call it a draw, Deuce? One pass for the fun of it?"

The man shook his head, angry. "No!"

Dirisha wanted to sigh, but held it. He wasn't very good at all, not as good as she'd first thought. He moved well enough sub rosa, but his resting was better than his active. That was unusual, but it happened. At this point, a better ronin would know where he stood and back off; otherwise, he'd be asking for grief.

Tea-skin yelled, a guttural grunt, and cross-stepped for his second pass. A kick this time, low, so he knew that much, but far too strong and slow. His foot came up from the floor, aimed at her pubis—

Dirisha V-stepped and was suddenly behind him. She cocked her right fist and fired the punch, slamming the two big knuckles into the man's back, over his left kidney. She heard the wind leave him as he moaned. Before he could recover, she lifted her left foot and stamped it against the back of his knee. Tea-skin's leg buckled and his knee cap smacked hard into the floor tiles; she heard the bone give. But he dove away and rolled, and when he came up, most of his weight was on one leg—not the one Dirisha had just crippled. He stared at her as though he couldn't understand who she was. She saw the pain twist his face.

There was no way Tea-skin had enough strength in the leg with the shattered kneecap to come at her again, not unless he hopped. It wasn't good, but it would do. Pain was the best way and following that, disabling injury. A little orthostat glue and the patella would be as good as new. But for now, Tea-skin was out of it. Dirisha said, "This dance is over, Deuce. Let me call the medics—"

Tea-skin jammed his hand into his tunic pocket and came out holding a single-blast shot tube. He swung it to point toward Dirisha—

Dirisha slapped her own hand onto her belt closure and ripped the kinzoku dart from its hidden sheath; the throw was a back-handed toss. She continued the flinging motion into a wide follow-through—that was important, the follow-through—and then dived after her hand, in a twisting back-flip. The gas charge in the shot tube went off and a spray of steel fanned the air where she had been a second earlier. One of the pellets slapped into her ankle, but glanced off the bone, leaving only small wounds. She landed hard, on her heels.

Dirisha stood and glanced down at Tea-skin. There was no pain on the man's face, no tension in his muscles. The kinzoku dart had buried itself in his forehead; the brain-shock must have killed him. Tea-skin had checked out, there was no longer anybody home.

Dirisha felt cold, a coldness which reached deeply into her and touched something hidden there. This was not what she wanted, this was not what she had trained nearly half her life to become: a killer, someone who could calmly wipe away another human with as little effort as throwing a sliver of steel at a target. Why hadn't he quit? It was obvious she was better than he had been, it was illogical, it was *stupid* for him to continue after he was beaten! She found herself angry at Tea-skin—she didn't even know his name—for being so stupid. It was his fault, not hers!

No. Dirisha knew she was wrong. Sure, she had to defend herself, but the other was just rationalization. She was too good to have taken the easy way. She could have risked herself more and maybe put him down without killing him, she knew it. She had done her technique correctly, but she had failed in her Art. Suddenly, she felt very tired, as if she had climbed some tall high-gee mountain into thin and life-less air.

She looked down at the corpse. Methodically, she re-trieved the stainless steel kinzoku dart and wiped away the blood. This was a bad world to kill somebody on, the au-thorities on Tembo were harsh and difficult to convince of innocence under the best of circumstances. They were less than fond of cults and Musashi players would receive little sympathy, either killed or killers. It would be wise to leave, and quickly. There was no official registration of Flex play-ers on Tembo, but it wouldn't take the cools long to figure out that Tea-skin had been such. Then, they'd be locked into suspects. Sure, it was self-dee, and any straight scan would back her story, but Dirisha had no desire to sit for some heavy-handed brain scrambler. People had been known to come out of such sessions wiped or nearly so—especially if the simadam running the scan didn't like the subject. It could happen easily on this world.

Tea-skin was heavy, but she managed to shoulder the body and walk with it. Corpses were always heavy, being literally dead weight with no muscle tone to help; Dirisha counted herself unfortunate to know such things.

People who passed on the nearly-deserted street glanced at Dirisha and her load briefly, if at all, and if they wondered about her, they did not do so aloud. She staggered along for two blocks before she found a refuse container large enough to accept a man-sized object. Too bad there were no public flash disposals on Tembo, a decidedly backward world compared to some. With a grunt, Dirisha heaved the body into the trash container and covered the unit. He'd be found soon enough, but probably not until she had time to leave the planet. She had enough stads in her account to travel nearly anywhere in the galaxy; money meant little to her and she seldom spent it on anything other than the barest items of survival. She could go to any world she wished, but—where did she want to go? She had learned as much of the local fighting art of T'umeaux as she cared to learn; after that, she had planned to try the wheelworld of Chiisai Tomadachi, orbiting Tomadachi itself in the Shin System. There was supposedly a variant of kaiatsu, which actually worked, being taught to a handful of students there. She had heard of voice-stun styles, but had never seen one which was truly effective. So, Chiisai?

As she left the alley in which she'd dumped the corpse of the man who'd attacked her, Dirisha felt that earlier weariness latch onto her again, as though some kind of malignant leech had attached itself to her spirit. Her *ki* seemed to drain away, leaving her exhausted. For a moment, the idea of continuing to play the Flex seemed too much to bear, to even consider. But what else could she do? Settle into some bodyguard job? Become a bouncer permanently? Set up a school and teach what she had learned? She could do that, she was good enough to attract the best students.

The face of a man dead nearly three years floated up from her memory. She smiled at the recollection. She'd liked Khadaji, liked working for him. A lot of people had been very surprised when they'd found out what he'd really been doing on Greaves. Dirisha had always suspected there was more to him than met the eye—he moved too well to be a simple pub owner on such a backrocket planet.

Dirisha kept the smile, but wondered why she was thinking about Khadaji now. Was it merely due to the death of Tea-skin, reminding her of another death? No, there was something else scratching at her memory. Something Khadaji had said to her once, shortly before he'd died. What was it, exactly? Something about being on some world in a few years . . . ah, she had it. He'd told her that Renault, also in the Shin System, would be a good place to be. A town called—what was it?—Complex? Vindox? No, it was . . . Simplex. Simplex-by-the-Sea. A place she could stretch herself, he'd said. What had he meant by that? What had he been trying to tell her?

Dirisha walked the dark street on Tembo, oblivious to her surroundings; she wondered about Khadaji's cryptic comments, made three years past. Simplex-by-the-Sea. It had a nice ring to it, it sounded peaceful and simple. Why not? She had no place else she had to go.

No place at all.

TWO ━━━━━━━━━━━━━━

THROUGH THE DENSECRIS window of the boxcar, Dirisha could see a world which looked to be made mostly of water. She had read the standard promoscan on the Bender ship from Tembo, so she knew a little about the place: Renault, fifth from the primary, one of six inhabited worlds in the Shin System. The world had three continents, a tug equal to one-point-one gravities, oxy around twenty percent. Eight million nine hundred and sixty thousand or so inhabitants, mostly human, with a scattering of mues for flavor. They produced a lot of trees and vegetables on Renault and some refined metals, but not much of the last. And not much else. A backwater place, just like her homeworld—a place Dirisha didn't like to think about. So—why was she here? Dropping in a rock-like glide from orbit, heading toward a

village on the southwestern coast of the smallest of the small
continents? Well, it was as good a place as any, until she
decided what she was going to do when she grew up.

Now, why had she thought that?

"Touchdown in six minutes," came the voice of the at-
tendant over the com. "Please engage your form-units to
landing mode."

Dirisha reached for the controls of her seat, trying to put
the thoughts she'd been having out of her mind.

The main spaceport for the hemisphere was on an artificial island twenty kilometers from shore—a precaution
taken on a number of worlds she'd visited—in case the
forerunners to modern boxcars, the rocket shuttles, decided
to explode on impact. Apparently such things had been
common in days past.

It was summer in the latitudes containing Simplex-by-
the-Sea, and it was hot. Even the breeze generated by the
speed of the ferry did little more than rearrange the sweat
drenching Dirisha. The ferry was old and it shuddered and
vibrated as it rode its uneven cushion of air across the
tropical water. Dirisha stood on the forward deck, feeling
the sun and air working on her tightly curled hair. Her
droptacts polarized automatically and cut a lot of the glare,
but it was still very bright. *Just like home*.

Ahead lay the village she was travelling to, a coastal
burg set around the perimeter of a bay girded with fishing
vessels. The boats wore strange rigging, wide V-shaped
poles strung with mesh—must be nets.

There were a number of small sailing craft leaning back
and forth, crisscrossing the bay. One of them, a tiny boat
of maybe eight or ten meters, seemed to be having trouble
aiming itself. The sailors were putting the boat directly into
the path of the ferry. As the two vessels neared, Dirisha

saw three people on the smaller boat, frantically pulling on ropes and gesturing wildly.

The air was rent by the ferry's warning horn, a deep, dinosaur-like blast.

The sailboat seemed to stall at the sound. It was directly ahead of the masive ferry and if it didn't move soon, it would be run down.

The sound of the ferry's engines changed, and Dirisha felt a slight tug as the big craft began to turn slightly to starboard. The dinosaur bellowed again, more insistently, but the smaller boat didn't seem to be able to move. Dirisha calculated the angle between the sailboat and the ferry and it looked to be critical for the sailors. The ferry was turning, but ponderously, and the three on the sailboat must know how precarious their position was.

They weren't going to make it, Dirisha saw. She stepped toward the metal railing at the deck's end and gripped it tightly, leaning over to stare at the sailboat.

With perhaps fifty meters left before impact, the sailboat suddenly seemed to lurch to one side; it would still be close—

Horn still blasting, the ferry slid by the sailboat, with less than five meters to spare. The bow wave and side slip of the air cushion rocked the little boat as if it were a chip of wood. The mast nearly touched the water as the boat heeled over and then, miraculously, righted itself. Dirisha was close enough to see the faces of the three people on the boat. Two men and a young woman. It looked as if the three were laughing. Then the boat was past her, still bouncing wildly in the turbulence of the ferry.

Maybe she'd laugh too, if she'd just missed death.

She had only a small bag containing the few possessions she owned, so it was easy enough to walk away from the ferry into the village of Simplex-by-the-Sea. A sleepy town, she decided, with most of the inhabitants staying inside perched in front of air conditioners or exchange strips, to beat the heat.

Now what? She was here, but she had no reason to be. She could look for a local pub, she figured, and maybe get a job as a bouncer. Or maybe just enjoy the sunshine for awhile, take long walks on the beach and watch the seabirds and the fishing ships shuttle back and forth. She had enough stads to play the rich woman—for awhile, at least. A vacation, a real vacation. She'd never had one of those before. There were times when she hadn't worked or hadn't been training, but those hadn't been vacations, only times between. She gripped the handle of her bag tighter and picked a direction—

"Hey, Dirisha!"

She dropped the case and spun quickly, startled. She slid into a defensive stance reflexively, her hands coming up in the oldest of her fighting systems, hard-style oppugnate. Nobody could know her here—!

Dirisha's green eyes widened in surprise and she grinned as she raised herself from her martial crouch. It was Bork!

The man she stared at was five meters away and walking toward her as if nothing on the planet could stop his progress. He was big, close to two meters tall, and on this world must have weighed nearly a hundred and twenty-five kilograms. His black hair had a little more gray in it, but his massive frame didn't look diminished—if anything, he looked larger and more muscular than when she'd seen him last. He wore loose-weave osmotic orthoskins and a pair of spetsdöds, one strapped to the back of each hand. Saval Bork, homomue, and once a bouncer in the Jade Flower on Greaves, as she had been. And a nice man.

Her smiled faded as the first question hit her: what was he doing here? Almost as quickly, the second question crowded into her mind—how did he know *she* was here? From his purposeful stride, it was obvious Bork did know, and that bothered Dirisha greatly.

Bork stopped next to her. "You look good, Dirisha. I'm glad to see you."

"I'm glad to see you, too, Bork, but I can't help but wonder why I *am* seeing you."

He nodded. Bork had the big man's temperament in a lot of ways but he wasn't stupid. "I didn't know you were coming until they told me to come collect you," he said, "but there are people who keep track of such things at the Villa."

"People? Villa?" She wasn't afraid, but she was definitely curious. There was no sense in Bork being here.

"Yes ma'am. Look, I've got a track waiting, I can tell you what I can on the way. This sun'll dry you out if you stand around too long. What say we ride?"

Dirisha thought about it for a few moments. She shrugged. Might as well; she had a feeling whatever Bork was into was the reason she'd come to this planet. She picked up her bag.

The track was a squarish vehicle which squatted on triple rails of what looked like weathered aluminum. Inside, the air was twenty degrees cooler. There were comfortable, if thin seats, and a dispensing unit for water sat under one long window. Bork activated a control and the track moved smoothly off, gathering speed until it was travelling at a good eighty or ninety klicks per hour.

Bork turned away from the control panel and grinned at Dirisha. "Automatic driver," he said. "I really am glad you're here. Sleel and Sister will be glad to see you, too."

"Sleel is here? And Sister Clamp? Come on, Bork, what is happening?"

Bork scratched at the back of his left hand with a thick

finger. "Stuff itches," he said, pointing at the plastic flesh which joined the spetsdöd to his own skin.

Dirisha repressed an urge to sigh. He was going to get to it in his own time, she supposed. She pointed at the spetsdöds. "Why are you wearing them? Is it dangerous here?"

Bork laughed. "Dangerous? Nah, I'm only carrying stingers. Everybody at the Villa has to wear them. Pen's second rule."

"Bork, you're giving me more questions when what I need is answers."

"Okay, it's like this. Sleel and Sister and I and a bunch of others are all working here, at the school. It's called Matador Villa and it's a kind of . . . training center put together in honor of a guy we used to work for, before he died."

"Emile?"

Bork's grin grew larger. "There are people who'd kill to be able to say that name the way you just did. Those of us who actually *knew* him are looked upon as kind of blessed."

"What are you talking about?"

"You remember what happened on Greaves."

"Of course I remember."

The rail car rounded a long curve at that moment, and the earth seemed to drop away to Dirisha's left. The sea was a hundred meters below all of a sudden, and the view was incredible; there was a pattern to the land ahead, almost like giant stair-steps to the water. She hadn't realized they'd been climbing. A series of buildings sat in the middle of one of the steps, terra cotta blocks against dry brown grass. It was hard to tell how large the complex was, there was little to scale it against, but it looked sizeable.

"Nice, huh? I always like this part of the trip."

"Let's get back to the story, Bork. Khadaji was part of

an underground resisting the Confed on Greaves and they finally caught up with him."

"Oh, there's much more than that. He was all by himself, did you know that?"

Dirisha nodded. "I heard that rumor."

"No rumor. Did you know what the military found out, after it all wound down? Our boss nailed over two thousand troopers, from bottom-grade line up to the Befalhavare Himself."

"I heard that, too. Not a rumor, I take it?"

"Nope. He did it, and every one of them with spetsdöds. And that during the whole time he was darting troopers all by himself, he never once blew a shot. Not one time. And that's according to the Confed military itself."

Dirisha blinked and stared at Bork. "I didn't know that."

"They call him The Man Who Never Missed, Dirisha; he's the inspiration and idol of all the students. One man, who stood up to the Confed, who only let himself be taken when he'd done what he set out to do. On some worlds, the name of Khadaji is like a prayer for resistance fighters."

"Is that what you're doing here, Bork? Training to be a resistance fighter?"

"Oh, no. I'm a student, learning to be a matador."

"What is a matador?"

"A bodyguard, Dirisha. Matadors are the best bodyguards there have ever been."

The woman stared at the big man. Was this what Khadaji had meant? Had he known somebody was setting up this— this school three years ago? He must have known, even as he'd known he wouldn't be around to see it. She'd asked him about Renault, but he'd told her then she wouldn't see him there. The man had obviously been much more than he had appeared to be, she had known that even on first meeting, but what was all this about?

The rail car approached the complex of buildings, slowing as it did so. Whatever was going on, Dirisha knew she was going to find out soon.

THREE ——————————————

THE SURFACE OF what appeared to be plastcrete was more than it seemed; it gave back a spring to Dirisha's steps as she followed Bork toward the largest of the buildings. Bork apparently noticed her interest, for he said, "Rockfoam. They use it on tracks and gym floors, like that."

Dirisha nodded. She didn't ask the obvious question: why such an expensive surface covering such a large outdoor area? Just ahead, she saw what appeared to be a dozen twisted lines of paint—no, they were patterns of footsteps, printed upon the surface. She stopped at the nearest trail and looked at it. The patterns were all identical, as far as she could tell. And from the way they'd been drawn, the angles and distances, it seemed apparent that the steps were to illustrate some artistic bent, rather than to be trod upon— certainly no normal human could follow the pattern and stay standing. She looked up at Bork, but he only grinned. "Pen'll tell you," he said.

Dirisha shrugged and followed the homomue into the shade of the largest building.

Where *was* everybody? Was the place deserted? So far, she'd seen no other people, save Bork.

Inside, the faded-brick facade gave way to stark white halls and high ceilings, with more of the rockfoam covering the floor. Bork led Dirisha through a wide hallway toward a set of what looked to be oak doors.

As they passed a side hall, a figure moved. Dirisha caught a gray blur in her peripheral vision and turned toward it—

It was a man—maybe a woman—dressed in a shroud which covered everything but its hands and eyes. As she watched, one of those hands came up suddenly, and pointed a finger at Bork. There came a cough of compressed gas—

Dirisha leaped to her right and slammed her shoulder into Bork, trying to move him aside. It was like smacking into a wall; she rebounded, turned the movement into a dive and hit the hard-but-soft floor into a roll and walk-out. She came up and reached for the kinzoku dart hidden in her belt clasp—

Something stung the back of Dirisha's hand, a sharp twinge no worse than a wasp might do. She ignored the sensation and continued to pull the dart free—

"Ah, *shit,* Pen!" Bork said. "It's not fair!"

Dirisha had the dart free and she cocked it by her left hip, for a side fling. But Bork's voice stopped her. She risked a quick glance at him.

The big man was rubbing his left arm with his right hand and shaking his head. He didn't look hurt, only disgusted.

Dirisha looked back at the figure in the gray robe and hood. It—he? she?—had both hands raised and both index fingers pointed at her. She knew if she were to risk the throw, she wouldn't make it before it fired. She relaxed slightly, allowing her hand to sag a few centimeters. The figure in gray immediately dropped both hands by its sides. It turned its head slightly and focused bright blue eyes on Bork. "First Rule?" it said. Or, rather, *he* said, for the voice was masculine. And odd-sounding, somehow.

Bork said, "But I was bringing her—"

"First Rule."

"'Students must be prepared for attack at any time.'" Bork said. "My fault."

"You thought you were safe because you weren't doing ordinary things, which is why the First Rule was created," the gray man said. "What do you consider a fair subtraction?"

"Ten points, I guess."

"Call it five. I don't want you to think I'm a tyrant."

Bork grinned. "Why, none of us would think that." He turned to look at Dirisha. "This is the guy I was telling you about. Meet Pen, Dirisha."

Bork left them alone in a room which was, Dirisha supposed, an office. Save for a table with a computer terminal and two chairs, the room was bare. There was a window which looked out into a courtyard lined with trees and bushes, but apparently Pen wasn't big on furniture. He sat in one of the chairs and Dirisha took the other.

"How did you know I was coming to Renault?" she asked, once they were alone.

The edges of the blue eyes crinkled and Dirisha knew Pen was smiling. He said, "When you used your credit tab to buy passage to Renault from Tembo, I was . . . informed."

"That's unlikely. You would have to have agents on fifty-six planets and over eighty wheelworlds to be certain of picking up such a transaction."

"Not really. Think about it for a moment."

Dirisha did so. The answer came suddenly. "You had me *watched?*"

Pen nodded.

Her first reaction was to jump from the chair, but she contained herself. She tried to sound calm when she spoke. "Why?"

"Emile Khadaji had great hopes for you," Pen said. "He thought you might find your way here one day. If you hadn't decided to come when you did, one of the school's agents would have eventually contacted you and asked you to do so."

"Again, 'Why?'"

"We want you to become a student here. And a teacher. Most of us do both, at this point. Pass on what we know, learn what we don't know."

"You say Emile wanted this?"

"Yes. He thought highly of you, along with some others he met along the way. I have a list of those he wanted us to contact. You were high on it."

"You have a list. Did you know him yourself?"

"I knew him. Long before you met on Greaves, I knew him."

"Well, this is all nice, but I really don't need lessons in how to become a bodyguard."

"No? I take it your protection of Bork in the hall was an example of your skill?"

Dirisha felt her face go hot. "I could have thrown the dart before I realized it was a game."

"Recall the sting you felt on your hand—the one holding the dart? If it had not been a game, you would have been down—if I had been using potent loads in my weapon."

Dirisha bit down on her anger. That was true enough. But it raised another question. "What if I hadn't noticed in time? I could have killed you, not knowing it was a test."

"Doubtful. Even with stinger ammunition, I would have been able to disable your hand so you would not have been able to complete the throw."

"How? I could have taken a sting or two—"

"But not a dozen stings, or more, perhaps."

Her inclination was to laugh or call him a braggart, but Dirisha did neither. His voice was matter-of-fact; not so much confident as assured. What he said was not a guess— in his own mind, at least—but an actuality. And, despite the concealing robe, there was a hint of Center control which showed through when they'd walked to the office. From what she had seen and what Bork had told her, Pen was some kind of adept. At what, Dirisha didn't know, but at *some*thing.

"You expected something different," Pen said, interrupting her thoughts.

"I suppose. I'm not sure what, but yes, something different."

"And you aren't particularly interested or impressed with our little operation."

Dirisha inclined her head briefly, acknowledging his perception.

He leaned forward slightly and brought the tips of his fingers together into a tent. "You're a ronin, playing the Musashi Flex, hoping to reach enlightenment. Maybe you can find it here."

Dirisha laughed. "Really? I've been to a dozen planets and nearly that many wheelworlds, studying. What makes you think you have something I couldn't find elsewhere?"

Pen stood, a move so smooth it seemed effortless. "If you would follow me."

He walked from the office without looking back, but Dirisha felt as if he were aware of her every movement.

They retraced the path Bork had used to bring her into the building. Once outside, Dirisha finally saw more people, a dozen or so, doing stretching exercises on the rockfoam. There were four women and eight men and they were dressed in loose-weave orthoskins, as Bork had been. There were enough variations in the cut and colors of the skins so they could not be called uniforms, but they were very similar.

Pen swept past the exercisers toward the lines of footsteps printed upon the spongy ground cover. When he reached the nearest, he stopped. "You are adept in a handful of martial arts, an expert in body control and movement," he said. "Can you walk the pattern?"

Dirisha stared at the complex layout of foot positions. She had played fugue now and again and the implication was clear enough: *I* can do it, can you?

She reached for her Center, felt the comfort there, and took a deep breath. Without a word, she stepped onto the first diagram and began to walk the pattern. The first five steps came easily. The sixth was more difficult, but she managed it. Years of training gave her the ability to make the seventh step, but she almost fell despite that. She managed to plant her foot upon the eighth step, but from there to the ninth was impossible. Dirisha knew her limits and she had reached them. She pivoted sharply to face Pen.

He nodded, and waved her aside with one hand. She moved, and watched very carefully as he approached the beginning of the pattern. She watched with all the zanshin perception she could muster, trying to see not only his feet but his entire body. She had spent years training, learning how to watch an opponent, to judge his moves exactly; but, even so, she had only the smallest inkling of how he did it. One moment and he was starting; another moment, and he was done. It was unbelievable and yet Dirisha was certain Pen had placed his feet precisely on each of the steps in the pattern; more, he had *danced* it and made it seem effortless. She was impressed. But she had to know something more important.

When Pen returned to stand in front of her, Dirisha said, "There are masters of a thing and then there are Masters of that same thing." More fugue, but simple enough so anyone with the smallest skill could follow it.

The edges of Pen's eyes crinkled, an obvious smile. He waved his hand at the group of people stretching nearby. "Pick one," he said. "Your choice."

Dirisha nodded. He knew fugue. She had challenged him to answer one of the classic martial problems: you can *do;* can you also *teach?* One of the problems with many great artists were that they were personally adept, but could not pass it on. There had been some greats—Lee, Sandoz, Villam—who had not been able to teach for shit.

On the face of it, her challenge had been answered. He must have been certain to offer her the option; still, Dirisha had learned to take little for granted. She turned to face the dozen people in orthoskins. She scanned the faces, looking for some hint of ineptitude. Nothing—wait. She stared hard at a young woman with blond hair cut like a cap. Her face looked familiar. Where had she seen it? She was certain she had . . .

It came to her suddenly. On the ferry, the near-collision with the tiny sail craft. That woman had been on the boat. Dirisha remembered her laughing face as the larger vessel had gone by, missing by scant meters. Surely that episode had been caused by a lack of attention or ability?

"Her," Dirisha said, nodding at the blonde.

Crinkle. "Ah, you have a good eye." Pen called out, "Geneva, would you demonstrate the Ninety-Seven Steps for Dirisha?"

The young woman smiled and gave Pen a small military bow. She walked calmly to the pattern, took a deep breath, and began her dance. She was not so smooth as Pen, nor as fast, but she made no missteps Dirisha could see from start to finish. When done, she bowed again, and walked back to her group. That she moved in her Center the entire time was a given. Dirisha nodded again. "What is the style called?"

"Sumito."

"I've heard of it. But I thought it was a religious system, taught only to priests."

"It was, formerly. The Siblings of the Shroud have given us a special dispensation to instruct it here."

"The dance is beautiful and complex," Dirisha said. "But how effective is it?"

Crinkle. "A personal demonstration?"

Dirisha nodded.

"You may attack or defend," Pen said.

"I'll defend."

"Wise."

For a long moment, neither moved. Dirisha stood in her basic relaxed no-stance stance, waiting. He would give some indication of his intentions, some tightening before he moved, and she would be ready—

He waved his hands, flicking his fingers back and forth and knotting them into a blur of weaving motions—

Dirisha didn't grin, but she wanted to. Some kind of kuji-kiri, maybe *Neshomezoygn*, organomechanical hypnosis. He'd have to do better than that, she knew how to avoid falling into the finger-trap—

But he was no longer there, he was *behind* her, in a motion so fast he almost had her. She spun, slightly off-balance, and lashed out with a quick snap kick. Pen danced away, as if doing the pattern of steps, as if he were alone and Dirisha no more than smoke to him.

Dirisha set herself in a side-stance, offering a smaller target, raising her hands to cover her face and body, but Pen didn't seem interested in striking or grabbing at her. He danced back and forth and his motions seemed an extension of his earlier hand trap. Suddenly Dirisha knew he was using his whole body as he had used the finger-weave. She looked away, using only her peripheral vision to track him—

There were two muted explosions; Dirisha jerked her gaze back to cover Pen. He was using his spetsdöds! Why didn't she feel the sting—?

In her moment of confusion, Pen moved. He twirled, seeming to move away, but his leg became a spinning blade, knocking her feet from under her. It was unexpected and Dirisha landed on her back, hard, despite the padded surface. She twisted and rolled, to avoid a follow-up, but she felt a soft touch on her temple before she could regain her feet.

She sighed as she stood, then bowed. The touch could have been harder and a shot to the temple was worth the victory.

Pen stood there, looking inscrutable in his robe and cowl. "More?"

She shook her head. "Not necessary. You know your stuff, Deuce. And judging from your students, you can teach it, too. Where do I sign?"

Pen laughed. What he said then warmed her, in a way the tropical heat could not begin to match. "Welcome home, Dirisha."

FOUR _____

THE BLONDE'S NAME was Geneva Echt and what she told Dirisha both intrigued and infuriated her. They stood in what was to be Dirisha's room, a large and well-lighted cube containing a bed, couch, table and chairs and a computer, as well as a small kitchen module and a sanitary fresher.

"Excuse me?"

"I said, 'You were set-up to pick me to walk the Ninety-Seven.'"

"You'll excuse me again, if I don't see how. There were almost a dozen others with you. I could have chosen any one of them just as easily."

"According to Pen, the psychology of a familiar face made it likely you'd go for me."

Dirisha regarded the other woman. She was fair-skinned and it made the idea of natural blondness seem valid. Geneva wasn't a small woman, though not nearly as large as Dirisha, and she seemed well-knit, tightly-muscled under the thin orthoskins. Her eyes were an icy gray, deep set and striking, and Dirisha figured Geneva's age at maybe five years less than her own, call her twenty-five. "The psychology sounds fine, but as far as Pen knew, you could hardly be a familiar face."

Geneva grinned, a happy smile which showed one slightly crooked tooth among all the straight ones.

Dirisha shook her head as she suddenly understood the reason for the smile. "It was no accident," she said flatly.

"It was one of the toughest pieces of sailing I've ever been involved in," Geneva said. "We had to make it look as if we didn't know what we were doing while we got close enough for you to see me clearly."

"That much I'll believe—I was fooled. I thought sure you were all fish food." She grinned, then had a thought. "But—how could he have known I was where I could see? I could have been asleep or in the fresher or reading a tape—"

Geneva walked to the computer set upon the long table under the window. She turned to face Dirisha, still smiling. "The school owns the ferry. We not only knew you were on it, we also knew precisely just where you were all the time."

Dirisha shook her head again, puzzled and still a little angry. "Why? Why go to all the trouble?"

Geneva shrugged. "I don't know, exactly. Nobody knows why Pen does most of what he does. There are others who run things, a council of sorts, but Pen is the real power at the Villa. He wanted to make some point, I suppose. Someday, in some class, he'll bring it up, to illustrate some teaching or other, and it'll be the perfect thing to say. I've only been here a year and a half, but I've learned that much about Pen: he takes the long view about things. Maybe it has to do with his training with the Siblings."

Dirisha considered that. "Am I the only one he—or the school—has had followed like this?"

"As nearly as I can tell, almost all of us had similar experiences. Maybe a couple of us found our way here on our own, but of the thirty-two students—thirty-three, now that you're here—I'd guess all had somebody watching them at one time or another."

"You are probably tired of me asking it by now, but—why?"

"You'll get to understand that after you've been here awhile, Dirisha. Why the training, why us, what we're supposed to do—"

"Hello."

Dirisha looked at the doorway and saw a slightly-built red-haired man of maybe fifty standing there, holding a long and flat case. He smiled at the two women.

Geneva said, "Red. You didn't waste any time."

"Second Rule, kid, it's my job."

"Dirisha, this is Red—I think he had a real name—"

"Lyle Gatridge," the man said, smiling at Dirisha. "But Red will do, until my hair falls out."

Dirisha looked at the man. For a moment, she didn't notice the pair of spetsdöds he wore, they seemed so natural on the backs of his hands. When she thought about it, she remembered that everyone she had seen so far at the school had worn such weapons. Red's face looked familiar, too.

Red put the case down on the table and opened it. Inside were a row of spetsdöds, ammunition magazines, and blocks of plastic flesh. The man looked carefully at Dirisha, then picked a small ampule of dark liquid from the case. He took one of the blocks of plastic flesh and squeezed the bottle's contents into the material, then began to knead the sub-

stance. The pinkish-tan of the flesh darkened as Dirisha
watched; Red kept adding color until the mass nearly matched
her skin tone.

"If you're making that for me, don't bother," Dirisha
said. "I'm well-armed with my own gear."

Red smiled but said nothing and Geneva turned from him
toward Dirisha. "Second Rule," she said. "'Students always
wear a spetsdöd.'"

"Pen's rules," Dirisha said. "Bork rattled on about them.
And Pen mentioned the first one when he shot Bork in the
hall. Just how many of these rules do I have to learn?"

"Stroke up your computer," Geneva said.

Dirisha strode to the table and rubbed one finger along
the pressure-sensitive ignition control. The holoprojic screen
ran through a color check, then lit with three lines:

1. STUDENTS MUST BE PREPARED FOR ATTACK AT ALL TIMES.
2. STUDENTS WILL WEAR A SPETSDÖD AT ALL TIMES.
3. THERE ARE NO RULES IN A FIGHT INVOLVING DEATH.

Dirisha turned to look at Geneva. The younger woman
shrugged. "That's it," she said. "Just the three. Very martial,
but then, that's what we're here to learn."

Dirisha nodded. She had no problem with the three lines,
they were standard enough fare; she'd seen similar things
in dojos on several worlds. The ceremonial bow on entering
meant one was supposed to be ready for anything from that
point on. Be ready, be armed, survive; simple enough.

"Students don't generally shoot at each other too much,"
Geneva said, "but they can. You get points if you win a
shoot, lose points if you don't—how many depends upon
the circumstances. They're only awarded by instructors.
Mostly, it's the instructors who will be blipping you when
you least expect it. Get used to the pop of a spetsdöd's dart,
you'll be feeling it fairly often. Keeps you awake in other-

wise boring after-lunch lectures on a hot afternoon, it does."

"It sounds like children playing games."

"Not according to Pen. You're only supposed to shoot somebody who, in your opinion, isn't alert and ready for you. If you shoot back and hit an assassin within a second of his hit, it's mutual slaying and you *both* lose points—that helps keep hot-shots from blasting everybody they see just for the dork of it."

"Who keeps score?"

"Everybody does. Honor system."

Dirisha nodded.

Red moved toward her, stretching the now-dark plastic flesh into thin sheets. "Hands," he said.

Dirisha extended her right hand and watched Red apply the material to the dorsal side. "I thought spetsdöds came equipped ready-to-wear with their own flesh."

Red looked at her, interested. "You know the weapon?"

"I've never used one, but I've seen them."

Red went back to smoothing the flesh. "Custom gives a better fit," he said. "We don't want somebody developing an allergy to the commercial mix, so we use a hypoallergenic that won't spark human or mue immune systems. Once it sets, you can pull it off and reapply it easily enough, but you always wear at least one piece, even in the fresher. You learn to eat with 'em, sleep with 'em, make love with 'em. You don't want to get careless, even loading blunt-tips. Especially while—ah—dallying with another in the altogether."

"I can see where that might be painful," Dirisha said. She kept a straight face as long as she could, then smiled.

Red seated the pair of aluminum devices on the still-warm artificial flesh. Dirisha moved her hands experimentally, adjusting to the new weight. Red watched her carefully.

He showed her how to load the magazines into the body

of the spetsdöd, and explained the firing mechanism. "It's simple; the trigger is in the tip of the barrel, just here. Electronic circuit, completed by application of the finger-nail. You point your index finger at your target and hyper-extend it, so—"

The spetsdöd coughed and the dart it fired chunked into the wall across the room.

"You'll start the basic class in the morning," Red continued, "and I don't expect anybody will be nasty enough to sting you on the first night, until you have some idea of how to shoot back."

"Pen might," Geneva said.

"Yeah, likely. If you see him, stay awake. If he points his finger at you, duck and start shooting as fast as you can."

"No point ducking," Geneva said. "If he shoots, he's gonna hit you. Probably on the hands, so you don't get a return shot off in time for mutual-kill. He's terrific, probably as good as Khadaji himself was."

Red laughed. "You might be exaggerating a little, Geneva."

"Maybe. He doesn't shoot at you much, does he?"

"Now and again."

"And how do those come out?"

Red shrugged, but said nothing.

After Red left, Geneva smiled and waved her own spets-döds at Dirisha. "You're technically fair game now. I'll wait until you've had a chance to check out the range and get used to these new toys, but after that, I might sting you myself. Points are points."

"Fair enough."

After a moment, Geneva's face grew more serious. "You knew him, didn't you?"

Dirisha misunderstood. "Red?"

"No, not Red. Khadaji."

"I worked for him. On Greaves."

Geneva's face took on a kind of awe. "So you knew him when he was the resistance?"

"All I knew was that he ran the Jade Flower, a rec-chem pub. I didn't know about the other. Nobody did, apparently."

"But you must have seen something special about him."

Dirisha thought about it for a second before she answered. Yes, he'd seemed a cut above the ordinary, he'd moved well, but either he was good at hiding it or not particularly *special*. But she sensed that wasn't what Geneva wanted to hear. So she said, "Yes, he was something special, all right."

"I envy you," the younger woman said. "I wish I could have met him. A man willing to take on an army alone, a man who won."

"In a manner of speaking, I suppose he won."

Geneva seemed startled. "What do you mean?"

"Well, he made an important point, surely. But they got him, in the end."

"He *allowed* them to take him out."

Dirisha shrugged. "Whichever. He isn't around any more; I was always taught that honor lies in staying alive to fight the good fight again."

Geneva was silent for a moment, and Dirisha got the impression she was angry at what she'd said. Well. She hadn't known Khadaji, only the legend which had apparently arisen after his death. Dirisha had seen the man, and he'd seemed human enough to her, whatever he managed to do. But she didn't want to make any enemies here. Not yet, anyway. So she said, "Red did a good job on these. I hardly know they're on."

Geneva seemed to shake her serious mood. "Oh, Red is good. If you see him watching you like he might sling a dart at you, better find an exit and get to it—he's deadly."

"Better than Pen?"

She seemed pleased at the question. "Nobody knows, for sure. They don't keep score between themselves. I figure the pair of them could probably take out the entire school in a shoot, if it came to that."

"Two men against thirty-three?"

Geneva nodded. "There's nothing official on record about Pen and Red, but the rumor is that Pen taught Khadaji himself sumito, years before Greaves. Red taught Khadaji how to use a spetsdöd."

Dirisha nodded, not speaking. It sounded as if there were some high-class talents working at Matador Villa. It ought to be interesting to see what they were teaching, and why.

"You know a lot about them," Dirisha said.

"Not really. But I have an advantage: Red is my father."

Geneva left and Dirisha spent a few minutes meditating, to clear her mind. When she finished, she gathered a handful of the stinger magazines and went to find the shooting range Red had spoken about. If people were going to be shooting at her any time soon, she wanted all the experience she could get with the weapon they and she would be using. There was no point in waiting for official training to begin, especially in light of the Third Rule.

After forty-five minutes of practice, Dirisha felt more comfortable with the spetsdöds. She was far from expert, but by the end of five magazines, she could hit a man-sized target at combat range every time, with either weapon. Tagging a target the size of hand—a moving hand, at that— would take a lot more practice, but at least she could fight back with some chance of success.

Back in her room, Dirisha slid her door shut and locked the closure mechanism. There was no key, and she found her thumbprint would unlatch the lock. Good; still, to be on the safe side, she set a portable squeal on the door. If

somebody tried to come through the entrance, the squeal
would let everybody for a long way know it.

Dirisha shucked her clothes and headed for the shower.
She passed in front of a full-length mirror in the fresher,
and paused to give herself a critical appraisal. 177 cm tall,
that was the same; 75 kilos, plus a couple, on this world.
Muscles still tight under her chocolate skin, hair cropped
short and tightly curled. Not bad for a battered old woman
of thirty-one T.S. She grinned. Naked, save for the spetsdöds, she stepped into the shower.

The hot water and ultrasonics washed away travel grime,
and she allowed the fatigue to steal over her. She started to
peel the spetsdöds off, to wash her hands, but stopped. True,
she was locked into her room, alone; still, it would be a
good habit to get into, keeping one on. She removed the
right spetsdöd, scrubbed and dried that hand, then reset the
plastic flesh before tending to the left hand. There was no
one to see, but Dirisha felt virtuous for her action.

After the warm air jets dried her, she finished her toilet
and headed for the bed.

In three minutes, Dirisha was asleep.

*She was being chased by a giant beast, some kind of
reptile; it screamed at her, its voice a high whine—*

Dirisha rolled from the bed, onto the floor, as she awoke.
The dream-reptile's screech was that of the squeal she'd
hung on her door: somebody was coming in.

The double cough of a pair of spetsdöds was almost
drowned by the screaming alarm, and the small vibrations
of the darts smacking into her bed could hardly be felt, as
Dirisha kept rolling. The angle was bad, but she managed
to swing her left arm around and point it in the general
direction of the open door. It was too dark to see anyone,
but Dirisha fired rapidly, four shots, and fanned her arm to
spread the pattern. She heard the first two darts thunk into

the wall to the left of the door—too high, dammit!—and knew the third and fourth shots had gone through the portal. Unless the attacker was a giant, those final two darts would have gone over his head. She dropped her arm slightly, to fire again, but the quick bite of a dart stung her on the inner thigh, just above her left knee.

Damn! It was dark, she couldn't see, so therefore it was likely her attacker couldn't see either, he would be shooting at the sound of her weapon. She could blast him and say he'd missed, nobody would know the truth . . .

She shook her head. *She* would know.

She sighed. "Okay, Deuce, you got me. Tell Pen to add points to your tally and take some away from mine."

The attacker must have found the squeal, for the racket died suddenly. In the dense quiet which followed, he spoke.

"If you had been a hair better with your spetsdöd, you would have tagged me; nobody else has ever gotten off four shots on the first night. One point, no more." The voice belonged to Pen. "You can sleep easy, now; I won't be back tonight."

Suddenly, he was gone; Dirisha felt him leave. She got up from the floor and went to slide the door shut. Even so, she kept her right spetsdöd at the ready; despite his promise, Dirisha also reset the squeal when she closed the door. Whatever else this place was going to be, she didn't think it would be dull.

FIVE ────────────────────

IN THE MORNING, they gave Dirisha a disease.

A medic in white orthoskins led the tall black woman to a form-chair in a private booth. "Lean back," he said, "I need to get at your right carotid. You'll feel a cold rush, but otherwise nothing. Takes about fifteen minutes for the program to run its course."

Dirisha nodded. She knew about viral-inject learning, though she hadn't been able to afford it until years after it would have been really useful. On her homeworld, a planet her mother had named her for, Dirisha's first education had been real-time at Sawa Mji Primary. Flat Town's basic was limited, and as much as the daughter of a good-time woman could expect, for free. At fifteen, Dirisha had found a compliant ship's officer; for use of her body, he had traded her a secondary ed disk he'd stolen from his freighter, the *Go*

Placid. Real-time, that disk was, and hard. Even with his help, it had taken two years to assimilate. After that, she had discovered the Arts, and so much of them was muscle memory that inject or hypnosia was of little use. You couldn't learn to punch from a tape, you had to *do* it—The pop of compressed gas startled Dirisha from her memories. In this case, the viral learning could be useful. She was a new student, there was a lot she needed to know, if she were to mesh with the classes already in progress. It wouldn't help her shoot straighter or walk the pattern, but it could fill in the academic gaps.

The medic looked at his thumbnail chronometer. "See you in a few minutes," he said.

Dirisha leaned back and the form-chair extruded itself to accomodate her, the machinery whirring so smoothly she could feel, but not hear it. This organization had money. Viral-inject was expensive, and a layout like this took more than a few stads. And, what was the ultimate purpose of all this? Not just high-tech bodyguards, surely—

Abruptly, Dirisha found herself sitting at a desk, surrounded by other people at identical desks, watching an empty lectern. After a moment, the shrouded figure of Pen appeared at the entrance to the room, and glided as though on wheels to the lectern. Dirisha grinned. Whoever had programed the ed virus had a sense of humor.

"Welcome to the Matador program," Pen said. "This session and the ones to follow are designed to introduce you to the scope and purpose of the training; you'll learn how and why we came to be, and basic information which will allow you to enter the mainstream classes at current levels." Pen paused a moment, then waved his hand. The room faded—

Dirisha sucked in a quick breath. The Jade Flower! The illusion seemed perfect: it was the same rec-chem pub she'd worked in three years past, as a bouncer. The soldiers sat

around the octagonal room, drinking or smoking or just
smiling around the edges of whatever chem they were stoned
on; there was Butch, the head tender; there was Anjue, the
doormaster; there was Khadaji himself, smiling and moving
through the throng; and there—there *she* was!

A pang of nostalgia hit her. It was as if she were actually
in the pub; she could feel the body heat of the troopers,
smell the cooked-cashew odor of flickstick smoke, see the
smallest detail.

Khadaji laughed at something a soldier said, then moved
to the center of the room. He seemed to grow a bit larger,
and the room around him seemed to fade as her former boss
stood there smiling. The background murmur of the place
died, and Dirisha heard Pen's voice.

"Emile Antoon Khadaji," Pen said, "former Jump-
trooper, former pubtender, former smuggler. At this point
in his life, he is rich, adept at many things, and filled with
a sense of purpose. Nearly a decade and a half earlier,
Khadaji had a moment of cosmic realization, at which time
he saw the fall of the Confederation and what part he must
play in it. Here, operating from a small pub on Greaves,
Khadaji has just begun his one-man resistance to the Confed."

The interior of the Jade Flower vanished; a moment later,
the image of Khadaji, standing alone against a backdrop of
trees and shrubs, appeared. He wore a set of plain tan orthoskins and a pair of spetsdöds. He spun, to face the woods,
as four troopers emerged. Each of the troopers was armed with
an explosive-slug carbine. The rattle of automatic fire tore the
quiet air; Khadaji snapped off two rounds, dived, rolled,
and came up firing again. The four soldiers fell, knotted
into balls as their muscles clenched involuntarily.

Spasm-poisoning, Dirisha remembered. The hospitals on
Greaves had been full of such wounded troopers. Six months,
it took for the stuff to wear off. Muscle relaxants didn't
work, it was CNS viral and self-replicating. No antidote.

Khadaji raised from his fighting crouch and turned to face his unseen audience. He smiled.

"Emile Antoon Khadaji," Pen said again. "One man who took on an army. When those troops he disabled began to recover and he knew he would be identified, Khadaji walked boldly into the office of the planet's military commander and paralyzed him, a final gesture.

"Shortly afterward, Khadaji allowed himself to be imploded, rather than taken alive."

Dirisha remembered. Sleel had been working and she had been off, but she had arrived in time to see the attack on the armored drug room of the Jade Flower. The super-condensed ball which had been an entire room and its contents had crashed through the pub's foundations and sank into the ground.

Pen's voice-over continued. "An inventory on Khadaji's ammunition supply revealed a perfect match with the number of troopers wounded during his resistance to the Confed. In six months of operation, Khadaji took out two thousand three hundred and eighty-eight of the Confed's finest soldiers. He never killed, he did it alone, and he never missed. Not once."

It was a propaganda piece, Dirisha knew, but even so, she felt a chill touch her. It *was* amazing, no matter how you looked at it. Total dedication.

The scene faded, like a holoproj deprived of power, and once again, Dirisha was in the classroom, watching the gray figure of Pen.

"Emile Khadaji was a rich man, when he undertook his mission against the Confed," Pen said. "He could have stayed within the system, wanting for nothing, respected and elite. He did not, for Khadaji knew the great dinosaur of the Confederation was dying. He sought to hasten its death, by being an example to free men and women—by showing them that resistance need not be thought of as futile.

If one man, alone, can do so much, what might a hundred dedicated people do?

"Ah, but there are other ways to fight. The power of education, the pen rather than the sword, is one. Change a tyrant's philosophy and you might avoid shooting him.

"Khadaji is our icon, but our methods are different. Those of you who have been selected to become matadors—the word is from an ancient language, it means 'killer'—shall serve not by killing the flesh, but by slaying those twisted ideas held by the Confed. The man or woman whose life is in your care will learn to trust you. You can whisper into important ears, pass on beliefs, perhaps change a pivotal mind. A seed planted may grow; from the dying body of the Confederation will eventually spring new powers. Perhaps, just perhaps, one of those powers may embody the ideas Khadaji knew to be truth: that mankind should be free; that initiation of deadly violence against another man or mue is wrong. This is why Khadaji chose the spetsdöd for his weapon; so, too, will you master the non-lethal ways of self-defense. That is our purpose."

Pen paused. He waved his hand again, and Dirisha floated in deep space, watching a giant, wheel-shaped ship sail by. An antique, the thing was, and it looked familiar, somehow. It was obviously pre-Bender in design, not stuck in the gravity well of a planet or star—wait, she recognized it now, it was—

"*Heaven Star*," Pen said. "The first extra-system ship built by humans, on its way to an epic voyage. Those of us who are matadors consider ourselves to be like this ship. Pioneers, of a sort, willing to risk everything for our cause. As a new student, you would not be here, did you not have certain talents or skills or similar dedication."

Pen stopped talking, and moved from behind the lectern. He walked down a short aisleway toward Dirisha. When he stood a few meters away, staring at her, he spoke again.

"You can leave at any time, if what we want is not what you want. Your memory will be left intact—we are not the Confed—and you may speak to us as you will. What we do here is not illegal, by the standards of this world or those of the Confederation. As long as we do not actively resist or counsel active resistance, the Confed allows some dissent, if only a small token."

Dirisha regarded the real-unreal Pen before her. She had never been political; her only desire, from the time she had left her mother, was to achieve martial enlightenment. The Confed could hang, for all Dirisha cared. But she was tired: tired of playing against the Musashi flexors; tired of drifting from world to world, searching for the next Art. This sumito Pen offered, the Ninety-Seven Steps, was something special, she could sense that. And there were people here who intrigued her: Pen, Red, Geneva, Bork. And more, they *wanted* her, enough to have kept tabs on her, to have her watched. Besides, augmenting her bodyguard skills would do her no harm. It was still as good a place as any.

"I'll stick around for awhile," she said.

Pen nodded.

The classroom swirled and vanished, to be replaced by a smaller room, with only a few students. Again, Pen stood in front of them.

"Once," he began, "I watched a class being taught to a group of small children. The subject was aikido, an ancient martial art which utilizes much inner energy, or *ki*. The instructor used an analogy to show internal versus external strength. '*Ki*,' he said, 'is much like an iceberg. There is the tip, which is visible, much as external strength which uses muscles; then, there is the internal strength, which is at once much greater and yet hidden.'

"At this point, the instructor drew a diagram of an iceberg, showing that nine-tenths of its mass was beneath a curly line, which stood for the surface of a sea. He went back over his analogy again, altering it slightly, gesturing as he spoke. The man was full of energy and enthusiasm, most eloquent, and I was quite impressed with his presentation of the concept of *ki*. When he had completed his explanation the second time, he said, 'Are there any questions?'

"A small boy, of perhaps four or five years T.S., raised his hand. The instructor smiled. 'Yes, Cos?'

"'What's an iceberg?'"

Some of the students around Dirisha laughed. She smiled, as Pen turned to look at her. "Do you understand the point of my long-winded story, then?"

Dirisha said, "I think so. One should not take anything for granted.

"Precisely," Pen said. "For the next few weeks, you will be exposed to very basic knowledge in politics, philosophy, psychology and history, among other less general subjects. Much of it may be a repetition of that which you already know; still, before we can proceed with your education, we must know that *you* know what an iceberg is."

The next weeks consisted of intensive class instruction in all the subjects Pen had mentioned. Some of it, Dirisha knew already—one could hardly travel around the civilized galaxy without learning first-hand basic politics, history and stellar-geography—but much of what she learned was new. The material was presented well, and Dirisha felt a sense of accomplishment as she assimilated the teachings.

She learned about the first L-5 colony, established around 2000 A.D.; more about *Heaven Star,* the first interstellar ship, sent out seventy years later; and, how, in 2193, the Bender Drive opened up the stars. When the dust of colonization settled, there were fifty-six inhabited planets and eighty-seven wheel worlds, and the Galactic Confederation had become the Law to which all must bow. Earth ruled all its children.

The material flowed, and Dirisha soaked it up. There was so much to learn, so much—

She opened her eyes, to see the tech smiling at her.

"Fifteen minutes," the tech said. "Any of it take?"

Dirisha blinked, to orient herself. It had not been like a dream, the viral learning; her memories seemed as real as if she had truly lived them. She nodded. "Yes. It took."

"Good. If you'll follow me, we need to get a routine physical. We have a Healy Diagnoster next cube over, it won't take a minute."

Actually, the exam took about forty-five seconds, and showed Dirisha to be in excellent health. As she dressed in the orthoskins she'd been given, Dirisha saw the tech's right index finger straighten slightly. She had seen enough people at the school to know that a curled forefinger was habitual, to keep from accidentally firing the spetsdöds everyone wore. It was enough warning for Dirisha to snap her hand through the sleeve of the orthoskins and point her own weapon at the tech's belly.

The tech grinned. "Just checking, to see if you were awake."

Dirisha returned the grin. "Awake enough so I think I can get you before you can twitch. I lost a point last night and I am tempted to make it up."

The tech's smile shrank a little.

"But I don't want you to have a bad morning. So what saw we part without exchanging stings?"

The tech's smile grew again. "Sounds good to me."

Dirisha walked down the long hall, feeling good. Her first real-time class was to be the pattern dance, the Ninety-Seven Steps. She had been thinking about it, and she thought she had an idea of how to manage the ninth step, the one she had failed to negotiate before. She would have to shift her center of gravity carefully, the stepping foot would have to be relaxed, and not tensed. She had watched Pen closely, and Geneva after him, and she was sure she could manage the ninth move, and perhaps the tenth. She didn't know where that would place her, among all the students who had much more practice, but she was used to being a beginner. Some of what she knew could be transferred to a new Art, but there was no shame in ignorance. If others had learned it, *she* could learn it: that had always been Dirisha's operational mode.

Geneva led a class of four students—two men and two women—through a series of stretching exercises on the outdoor rockfoam. The morning sun was bright, and it was already warm enough to cause the students to sweat heavily.

Geneva smiled at the black woman, and waved her over.

"This is the advanced class," Geneva said. "You'll be working out with them."

Dirisha shook her head. "I'm just a beginner."

Geneva laughed, as did the four students.

"Something funny?"

Geneva nodded. "You managed eight steps on your first try; the average is three, a good score is five, and Khadaji himself only did six his first time. Aside from Pen, only two of us can walk the Ninety-Seven to the end. Red can't, Bork can't. Nobody ever got to eight on her first try before, at least not here. It took me a week to get to eight, and before you, I was the fastest."

"You must be joking."

"Not me, sister Dirisha. You are *good*."

"I still think Pen took a big risk, letting me pick somebody else to walk the pattern, only two chances out of all the students—"

"Only one, actually," Geneva said, still grinning. "Mayli Wu wasn't there."

Mayli Wu? Where had she heard that name before? Dirisha scanned her memory. She knew the name, but where was it from . . . ? She had it. She knew Mayli Wu, but under a different name. "Sister Clamp?"

"Our head medic," Geneva said. "And she teaches sexual techniques and the psychology of love. She's the other one who can walk the pattern."

Dirisha shook her head. "Why did he take the chance?"

"He wanted to impress you. And, besides, Pen doesn't really take very many chances. You picked me, didn't you?"

Dirisha nodded, not speaking.

"Okay, let's stretch, we'll do PNF for awhile. Pair up."

Geneva touched Dirisha softly on the shoulder. "I'll work with you, if that's all right?"

Dirisha nodded, and smiled at the blonde. "Fine."

As Geneva helped her do the PNF—proprioceptive neuromuscular facilitation—stretching, Dirisha felt that surge of wonder again. These people seemed to know exactly what they were doing; the ease with which she had been manipulated scared her. She resolved to do a little extra research on her own.

SIX ─────────────────

RED TOSSED A cube the size of a thumbtip at Dirisha. She caught the heavy chunk of translucent plastic easily and regarded it. "Looks like a stad cube," she said.

Red nodded. "Some of the locals aren't tied into the planetcom net, so they won't be able to get your credit file. You need something from one of the bandit-merchants, use that."

They were standing in the holoproj booth at the end of the spetsdöd range. Red triggered the control: a pair of short, dark mues ran down an alley toward Dirisha. One of them jerked a hand wand from his tunic, while the second one pulled a throwing steel. Dirisha snapped her right hand up and fired, twice. The pair of computer-animated attackers stumbled very realistically and fell, knotted as if by Spasm poisoning.

"So, we get an allowance for this training?"

Red shook his head, smiling. "Nope. You get *paid*, love. You're a student and a teacher. Local taxes and bribes are deducted from your stipend, just like you were a fisher or a tech." Red looked at the computer simulacrum, then at his control board. "Why'd you shoot the one with the hand wand first? At ten meters, the steel is a deadlier weapon. The wand's pulse is for close work, he was three meters away from his range."

Dirisha shrugged. "The steel is slow, I could have ducked or danced it. The wand's pulse is like a shotgun—if he'd got a shot off, I'd have no place to go. And the wand could have been boosted."

Red smiled, and nodded. "So, I'm wasting my time, trying to teach you combat principles? All you need to do is practice shooting? Could you have hit the steel in the air?"

Dirisha considered it. "No. Not yet. Outside of a lucky shot." She rolled the plastic cube with her thumb and fore-finger. "I have enough standards to live here forever," she said, "what with the school supplying food and rooms. But just out of curiosity, what are we dragging in here?"

"Not much," Red said, his face bland. "Two thousand stads . . . a week."

"What?" Dirisha was sure she'd heard him wrong.

"Hundred thousand a year, give or take."

"Sweet Buddha's left nut!"

"You'll make more when you go to work on your own. Pen plans to charge a quarter million a year for a fully-trained matador. Refundable if the client is assassinated under our protection. The school will keep ten percent, the rest belongs to the matador. Or, in your case, the matadora."

"He really thinks he can get that kind of money for a *body*guard?"

Red laughed. "We've got a waiting list a parsec long,

Dirisha. The first graduates won't be ready for maybe three more years, and there's been a semi-sub rosa ad campaign going for the last year—people with enough stads and power are pounding at our doors, figuratively speaking."

One of the simulacrum mues suddenly leaped to his feet and lurched at Dirisha. The one with the throwing steel. He drew back and whipped the triple-pointed weapon at Dirisha. She dropped, one leg extending to the side, in a Dweller-at-Sea's-Floor pose. She fired both spetsdöds at the mue; the spinning steel whirled over her head, missing by maybe five centimeters. The mue did a back handspring, without using his hands. The sound of the twirling steel was joined by that of the mue's neck snapping.

Dirisha rose from her pose, and shook her head at Red. "You cheat. I got him fair the first time."

"You know what kind of mue that was?"

Dirisha looked at the downed figures.

"Looks like one of the enhanced-darkers. Bruna System, maybe, from Farbis?"

"Right system, wrong world. Muta Kato."

"Okay, so I missed the planet. Why is it important?"

"Think about what they export from Muta Kato."

Dirisha thought about it. Somewhere in her real-time training during the last two weeks, she must have heard something about the mutant humans developed for Muta Kato; otherwise, Red wouldn't be making a big deal of it. What came from there? Wines, some kind of exotic art with living plants, drugs. Yes, now she recalled: there was some kind of potent shellfish virus, used in surgery...

"Oh, damn!" She pointed her spetsdöd at the other mue, the one with the hand wand, and fired three times. The thunk! of the pellets hitting him seemed loud in the narrow room.

Red's grin widened.

"They're partially immune to Spasm," she said. "Something to do with being stung by the poison shellfish they harvest for drugs."

"Good for you. You see a Muta Katoan coming at you, you always shoot him three times—otherwise, he'll get up and kill you, you're only using Spasm."

"Damn, damn!"

"And don't pay too much attention to me when I tell you I can't teach you anything," Red said. "Hubris won't serve you very well."

"I stand taken down a few meters," Dirisha said. "And thanks."

In the hall outside the shooting range, Geneva Echt ran past. She paused, and waved to Dirisha. "Come on," Geneva said. "Bork is going to try for the record today."

Dirisha looked at Red.

"Go," he said. "You don't want to miss this."

Saval Bork had shed his orthoskins, and stood naked except for a scrotal support, lifting belt, and half-fingered gloves and spetsdöds. Legs spread wide, Bork looked as if he could be the model for the Farnese Hercules, only bigger. Nearly two meters tall and weighing a hundred and twenty five kilos, Bork had muscles of a size and density unlike any Dirisha had ever seen. He was a heavy-gee child, and he had kept his tone using "organic" steel, instead of magnetic fields or electrostim.

As Bork stood meditating among the racks of barbells, Dirisha again marvelled at his physique. She had seen him work out when they'd been bouncers in Khadaji's pub, and that had only been his normal maintainence routine; today, he was going to try for something more.

Geneva edged over a few centimeters, to stand closer to Dirisha. "He looks as if he could pick himself up with one hand," the blonde said in a whisper.

"I wouldn't bet against it, if he said he could do it."

Dirisha's voice was also quiet. "Did he ever tell you how we got to be bouncers at the Jade Flower?"

Dirisha could feel the other woman's interest perk.

"No. He doesn't talk much about himself. What happened?"

"Emile didn't want the troopers causing a fuss in the pub, so he nailed the furniture down—bolted the stools and tables to the floor. That way, nobody'd be bashing heads and getting the place shifted off-limits. To get the job, you had to move one of the bolted-down stools."

Geneva stood as though in a trance. Stories of the hero, Dirisha thought, guaranteed to hold the faithful spellbound.

"So, Emile had the applicants come in, one at a time. First guy never even got started, Khadaji waved him off when he saw the guy's form. Then Sleel arrived." Dirisha watched Bork take a deep breath, then cross his arms. The ripples under the man's skin made him look so muscularly alive that the hairs on her neck stirred. "By the way, where is Sleel? He's supposed to be here."

"Off planet, doing something for Pen. He'll be back in a week or two. Finish the story, Bork is almost ready."

Dirisha grinned. Hell of a narrative hook she had. "Yeah, well, Sleel struts in like he does, cock of the galaxy, and Emile gives him the rif: the stool is bolted, he wants the bolts tested, see if you can move it."

Bork took another breath, let it out, and spread his arms wide.

"And?"

"And Sleel squatted and set himself and had at it. You must know how Sleel operates."

"Yes, he's . . . ah . . . single-minded."

Dirisha laughed quietly. "You sleep with him yet?"

Geneva nodded, smiling. "I hadn't intended to, but, well . . . ah . . ."

"Yeah, I know, he's single-minded."

"He's very energetic," Geneva said. "And . . . ah, rather . . . potent."

"What I hear," Dirisha said. "Anyway, Sleel about busted a gut, but he wrenched the stool loose."

"He told you about it?"

"No, I was watching. Hidden. I like to know the territory I plan to walk, so I found a way in and a place to blend into."

Bork took another deep breath and exhaled slowly.

"Okay, so then what?"

"Then, I took off. Found a place that sold tables and stools like the one in the Jade Flower. Did some examining of the construction. Some figuring. Then I went back and slipped into the pub. About that time, Bork was up."

As though the whisper of his name was a signal, Saval Bork shook himself and walked to the massive padded bench two meters away. A polychrome bar with plates packed onto both ends lay across a pair of Y-supports. Bork sat on the bench, took a few breaths, then lay backward, under the bar. He nodded once, and somebody clicked the repel pressors on; the hum and low drone of the safety field was the only sound in the quiet exercise room. Bork closed his eyes, and reached up to lightly touch the bar with his fingertips. He stroked the polychrome flexsteel gently.

Geneva's voice was so faint Dirisha could barely hear it. "So, what happened at the Jade Flower?"

Dirisha held her grin, watching Bork. "Oh, Emile told Bork he had a stool he needed moved. Bork reached out and grabbed the thing with one hand and moved it for him."

"With one hand?"

"As if the thing weren't screwed to the floor; as if it took no more effort than straightening his tunic. Took him two seconds; it was like he didn't understand why it wouldn't move, at first, then he shrugged and just *moved* it."

"Damn."

"Yep. And Bork says, 'Where do you want it?', and Khadaji says, 'Anywhere. Can you start work in a week?'"

Geneva grinned. "I'm impressed. But—what about you? How did you manage to—?"

"Shhh." Dirisha pointed at Bork. He had wrapped his hands around the bar, and was beginning the bench press. The safety field would allow him to lower the weight slowly, Dirisha knew, but were he to drop it, it would hang for a few seconds before it began to settle, allowing Bork to scoot out from beneath it safely.

Bork straightened his arms, and the barbell rose from its supports, until the big mue's arms were locked; then, he began to slowly lower the bar toward his chest. Dirisha had been trying to figure out how much weight he was using. Each of the large steel plates was fifty kilos; there were four of them, two hundred kilos, plus a little more for the hair above one gee that Renault had. Then there were two more plates on each side, Dirisha thought they went twenty kilos each, that made it two-eighty—

Bork grunted as the bar touched his thick pectorals. He kept his back flat on the bench, no arch, and he did not bounce the weight. His face turned a darker shade of red as the bar began to slowly rise.

—Two-eighty, plus the bar itself, which weighed—what?—twenty? twenty-five kilos? Call it three hundred kilos, minimum, probably closer to three-twenty. Incredible, that a man or mue could move that amount of weight, using only the muscles of the upper body, the chest, shoulders, and arms...

The weight reached its apex, and stopped. The ten students and instructors watching cheered. Bork had done it; he'd broken not only his own record but the planet-wide record, too.

Then, as Dirisha and the others watched, astounded, Bork lowered the weight—not to the supports—but to his chest again.

It was only after he'd pressed the thing three times that he allowed it to fall into its cradle. When he sat up, he was grinning. "So much for that," he said. "What say we work out now?"

Dirisha felt Geneva's touch on her arm, a quick clamp of fingers which transferred all manner of information to her: admiration, awe, envy and . . . lust. Dirisha had no problem relating to any of those. She was, by choice, nearly celibate; Bork's effort made her feel desire, and she wondered at its primal nature, that it could touch her so deeply. More importantly, the feel of Geneva's hand on her arm seemed altogether too comfortable.

SEVEN ────────────────────

HER DOOR CHIME sounded as Dirisha stepped from the warm air of her fresher's dryer. She checked to see that both spetsdöds were seated properly as she padded naked across the floor to the entrance. Holding her right hand so her weapon pointed at groin level, she slid the door open.

Geneva stood there, palms toward Dirisha, fingers pointed at the ceiling. Both women grinned.

Dirisha stepped back and allowed the blonde to enter her cube. The dryer had not quite evaporated all the moisture of her shower, and the coolness felt good on her bare skin.

Geneva glanced at Dirisha appraisingly. "You look good," she said. Her voice carried admiration, along with a faint undertone of something else Dirisha couldn't place.

"Thanks. Nice to have something to show after all the years of work. What's up?"

Geneva walked to the bed and flopped onto it. She took
a deep breath and blew it out. "Sleel is back. Turns out Pen
sent him for some kind of bandit economic package he wants
us to study—it's in the computer, and we're supposed to
have read it by 0700 tomorrow."

Dirisha walked to her closet and pulled a set of orthoskins
from the rack. She began to tug the clothing on, noticing
as she did so Geneva's interested glance.

"It's a dork, I looked at it," the woman on the bed said.
"Forty thousand words of esoteric objectivistic capitalism,
by somebody named Veelson, a Rand-Brandonist from one
of the early wheelworlds, I think. A real sleeping potion.
I dread reading it."

"Sounds like fun. I wonder why Pen wants us to bother?"

"Who knows? Pen's got a mind more twisted than a
juniper bonsai. He's got some reason, you can be sure."

Geneva sat up on the bed, leaned forward, and stretched.
She rubbed at the back of her neck with one hand, then
moved her head slightly back and forth in a roll.

"Problem?"

Geneva continued the roll, stretching. "Sparring with Pen
this morning, I tried something tricky. It didn't work."

Dirisha laughed. "Nothing ever works on Pen."

"Tell me. Anyway, I wound up ground-thunking at an
angle I could have done without. I'm a little sore."

Dirisha finished dressing. "We'd better hurry. Class starts
in five minutes."

Geneva came up from the bed in a smooth motion, set
in her Center, in perfect balance. "Yeah, this'll be interesting. Mayli is supposed to show us something special
today, so I hear."

"More physiology?"

"*Applied* physiology, is the scut. Sexual how-to."

"Could be interesting, all right."

"I also hear she's using Bork to demonstrate it."

Both women grinned again. Dirisha said, "That could be *real* interesting."

When she had worked in the Jade Flower on Greaves, Mayli Wu had been known as Sister Clamp; she had been the most requested prostitute in the pub, if not the city, and stories of her skills and physical capabilities kept a line of customers waiting whenever she worked. Dirisha had never been with her, but she recalled the story of how Sleel had tried to outlast Sister. He'd wound up being treated for phlebitis of his penis—by Sister, who had been a full-fledged medic before she'd gone into another line of work.

If half the stories were true, nobody was better qualified to teach advanced sexual techniques than Mayli Wu.

Ten students sat in desks around the auditorium, looking down on the sunken demo platform where the woman stood next to Saval Bork.

At first glance, Mayli seemed nothing special. She was a short, dark, vaguely oriental woman of standard or mildly altered stock; black hair, cut very short, capped her head; her eyes were violet or black, and she was thin—hardly the form one tended to associate with a voluptuary—almost boyish in her configuration. Not a person most would see as an object of passionate desire, Dirisha felt, judging by her experience in such matters. Then again, there was something about the way the woman stood, the angle of her stance, her gestures, which invited a second look. Even this far away, the pull was apparent, to anybody with sense enough to pay attention. Up close, Dirisha knew Mayli was compelling, but for no reason easily discernable. Body language, pheromones, something was there. Even though sex had been a very small part of Dirisha's life since she'd left her homeworld, she had been tempted to try Sister

Clamp when they'd first met; there was something there. . . .

Mayli began to speak. A focused microcaster transmitted her voice clearly around the room.

"We've talked about anatomy and physiology," she said. "You should now know about hormones, pheromones, excitation response, psychology of orgasm and pretty much what goes where."

A few voices laughed. Saval Bork looked uncomfortable. He shifted his weight from one foot to another.

"But all that is merely background. There are more important things about sex, about lovemaking. Anybody want to hazard a guess as to what I'm getting at?"

"Technique," somebody said. The word exuded confidence.

Dirisha turned, to see the source of the comment, but she had already recognized the voice: Sleel, her former co-bouncer at the Jade Flower: Sleel, who fancied himself the leading contender for the galaxy's greatest everything.

Dirisha chuckled, but for a different reason than most of the class. Sleel saw her, and nodded, raising one finger in a mock salute. If there were gods, they must know Sleel had tried to get to Dirisha often enough. He had never managed it; he had never stopped trying.

Mayli's smile was radiant. "What would I do without you, Sleel?"

Sleel returned the smile, cat-full-of-canary.

"You're wrong, of course. Technique is an aid to the art, but not the essence. What really makes it work?"

Dirisha was looking at Geneva when the blonde spoke, as if she had known somehow Geneva would answer.

"Love," Geneva said.

Only Sleel laughed this time. Everyone else was waching Mayli, who beamed at Geneva as though she had just revealed the biggest secret in all the Universe.

"Love," Mayli repeated. "Love. There you have it, all

in a word. Love is what makes it work. You can be crippled, ugly, or stupid; if somebody loves you, it doesn't matter. I tell you this from experience: there is no sensation to compare with being loved, or with loving. Inept sex, under the gleam of love, can be more wonderful than sex with the best technician, without love. It might not be as exciting or as nerve-tingling, but it is ultimately more satisfying.

"Love carries with it trust, and trust allows relaxation, caring, all the things which love conjures within its magic web."

"Define 'love' for me, then," Sleel said.

Mayli reached out and touched Bork's thick arm. The big man seemed to grow even bigger. He blushed.

"Here you see it," Mayli said. "Bork loves me; I love him. Oh, I can tell you the words—endearment, desire, attachment, lust, admiration, tenderness, altruism—and I can define each term, but it won't convey the true sense of it, what love is. I'm not sure that part can be taught. I *do* think learning how to love is possible; one can learn how to listen and really hear; one can learn how to look and really see; one can learn how to touch, and really feel.

"I speak not of lust, sometimes mistaken for love, nor am I confusing love with romantic self-delusion. There is nothing wrong with lust or romance, save what they lack, compared to love."

Sleel shook his head, but said nothing. A skeptic to the core, Dirisha had once felt, but she had changed her mind. At the end, in the Jade Flower, Sleel had shown his true colors: he was a frustrated romantic, a thing often mistaken for skepticism.

Mayli turned to Bork, and took his hand in both of hers. "Bork, would you kiss me?"

Bork looked at the ten students watching from the auditorium, then back at Mayli. He nodded. "If you want."

"I want."

Bork bent and carefully wrapped his arms around the small woman. He lifted her more gently than Dirisha would have thought possible, and touched his parted lips to hers.

Dirisha imagined she could feel the heat of their passion even where she sat, ten meters away. The kiss was soft and slow, and Dirisha found she was holding her breath. Her own heart beat faster, and she felt somehow. . . . privileged to be watching this tender act. It was, in its way, more stirring than any pornographic presentation could have been. She could not have said why.

Mayli broke the kiss; Bork lowered her to the ground and stood looking embarrassed. "Thank you," she said to the big man.

He grinned. "You're welcome."

Mayli looked at Bork with a singleness of mind which made Dirisha feel as if she were invading their privacy. Then the woman turned to face the audience.

"Love," she said. "That's all for today."

As Dirisha rose, she saw Geneva looking at her, and she felt a stirring akin to that she'd felt when Bork and Mayli had kissed. Dirisha glanced away, feeling uncomfortable, but she saw Sleel standing there, arms crossed. She expected to see his perpetual sneer, but even Sleel looked as if he had been affected by the demonstration; he seemed lost in thought, a million klicks away.

When Dirisha started for her cube, she passed within a meter of Geneva. The closeness now made Dirisha uncomfortable; she felt confused, somehow, as if she had just learned something of great import, but couldn't quite say what it was. It had only been a simple *kiss*, for Chang's sake—!

"Dirisha?" Geneva looked at her and raised one eyebrow.

"Yes?"

Geneva had her spetsdöd raised. "Pop," she said.

"Gotcha." But the expected sting did not come. Geneva lowered the weapon.

"You had me," Dirisha said. "I was completely lax, I admit it. Why didn't you shoot?"

Geneva's voice was soft when she spoke. "Ask Mayli."

Dirisha shook her head gently. "Oh, shit," she said. "Shit, shit, shit." Dirisha was overwhelmed by the suddenness of her emotion; she felt more vulnerable now than she had in almost fifteen years, and she didn't want to feel that way. "I—I don't think I can be what you want," she said. "There's too much vacuum past the port, too many years of being what I am—"

"But you feel it," Geneva said.

"I feel *some*thing . . ."

Geneva touched the bigger woman's wrist with her fingertips. The blonde's face was radiant, and she smiled.

"Shit," Dirisha said softly. "Oh, shit."

They lay entwined in Dirisha's bed, bare skin touching at legs and arms and breasts; Dirisha kissed Geneva's neck, blowing softly on the damp spot afterward. It had been a long twenty minutes so far, with hesitant explorations of each other's bodies, touching, kissing, stroking—

Geneva slid downward, and twirled her tongue around Dirisha's left nipple in a slow circle. Dirisha felt a warm rush; she stroked Geneva's hair, patting her head gently.

The blonde moved farther down Dirisha's body, darting her lips and tongue against the chocolate skin, raising goose-bumps.

Dirisha sighed, and parted her legs as Geneva moved her attentions lower; the warm tongue met damp vaginal lips, and traced them so softly it was like the touch of a feather. Dirisha groaned at the sensation.

After five minutes of Geneva's expert cunnilingus, however, Dirisha rubbed softly at the blond hair. "Hey," she said, "why don't you come back up here?"

Geneva shook her head, and spoke into Dirisha's mons. "Not done yet."

"You're doing fine, but I can't let go, hon. Come on."

Dirisha tugged at Geneva, pulling her upward until they could embrace and the bigger woman could kiss the smaller's throat. "My turn," she said, sliding her body against Geneva's.

The salt musk tasted just fine; it only took a few moments before Geneva was shuddering and spasming against Dirisha's face, clutching tightly to her head as she arched her back. "Oh! Oh, yes!"

They lay side by side, holding hands. Geneva squeezed Dirisha's fingers. "I love you," she said.

Dirisha sighed. "I know. I wish you didn't."

"Why? You don't have to feel that way about me, it's enough that I do."

Dirisha smiled, and leaned over to kiss Geneva's forehead. "You deserve better, hon. I don't know if I can ever get to that place. There's too much you don't know about, riding my shadow, too much I have tied up and hidden away in my head. I like you, I trust you, as much as I can, I don't feel threatened by you—nobody has gotten this close to me since I left my homeworld. But . . . I—I just don't know."

"Can you tell me about it? Maybe I can help, somehow."

Dirisha looked at the gray eyes and angelic face of the woman lying next to her, and sighed. "It's a dull story, hon. Not much interesting in where I came from, and why."

"Please. I'd like to hear it."

"All right. For what it's worth, I'll tell you. . . ."

EIGHT _____

THE PORT OF Sawa Mji baked under the hard glare of the sun called Ndama; Flat Town in the tropical summer, leached of color, the air so damp sweat wouldn't evaporate. The fifteen year-old girl felt the cheap cotton coverlittle she wore sticking to her flesh like a wet second skin.

It was going to get wetter, too, Dirisha saw. A thunderstorm was building to the West, and it wouldn't be long before it swept over Flat Town like a broom. Shitso, why did Tundu and Zawadi have to have the fucking room every afternoon?

Involuntarily, Dirisha grinned. It wasn't the room doing the fucking, it was her mother and half sister. With some dink-dong from a third class freighter, at guild minimum and no tip, she'd bet.

Dirisha started thinking about a place to sit out the rain.

She'd used up her chits for the library for the week; Kivu's
Emporium would be full of shippers who would go for her
like dogs around a bitch in heat, she didn't want to spend
an hour fending them off; the stolen admit cube she'd been
using to get into the retail shops was blank-washed by now.
Damn. Who did she know who wasn't working today? Nobody, she could think of; the ships were in, and in a port
town, that was stads in your pocket, gris-gris for your credit
cube. If you were sixteen, that is. You couldn't join any of
the guilds until you hit sixteen T.S. Oh, yeah, Dirisha thought,
she could freelance, and take her chances on brain-stir or
ice-time, when they caught her at it. No thanks, Deuce, bye
that one. She'd wait another year and do it right, become
a good-time girl like her mother and sister Zawadi. The
merchandise was still pretty fresh, she had given it away a
few times for fun or black market stuff, but the shippers
liked it young—

"Hello," a man said. "Kinda hot to be standing in the
sunshine, isn't it?"

Dirisha jumped at the voice. Through slitted lids, she
looked at the man. A shipper, what else? and a young one.
Dirisha figured him for a first-travel caddie, officer material,
if he stuck with it. Pale skin, he had, hair so black it looked
almost blue, cut in spike-and-locks, watery blue eyes. Not
bad looking, but nothing special.

"I'm too young, shippie. Come see me in a year."

He blushed. *Blushed!* And said, "N–no, I—I—didn't
mean, that is, I—I—don't want—"

Dirisha grinned. "You don't want me?" She tried to sound
hurt. "You think I'm ugly?"

"No, you're beautiful! I mean . . . that is, I . . ." he waved
his hands helplessly.

Dirisha laughed. Poor kid, he probably didn't know where
his dork *was* much less what to *do* with it. She could manage
him just fine.

She reached out and touched his arm, caught it with her sweaty fingers, feeling the richness of his synlin coverall as she tugged at him. "Come on, you're right, Deuce. It's too hot to be outside and besides, it's gonna rain in about five minutes. Let's go to the Emporium and you can buy me something cool to drink."

He smiled at her and nodded. "My name is Colin."

"Good for you, Colin. I'm Dirisha, like the planet."

"You were named after this world?"

"Nah, Deuce, they named *it* after me. What do you think?"

He blushed again, and shook his head.

Dirisha's grin broadened. Not only was he her ticket to shelter from the storm, he was a *sarhg*-seed, fresh as a ten-year-old from the country. She could get something to drink, some flickstick toke, and a meal out of him, without letting him touch her. And if she touched *him*, why, he'd probably blow out before he got within a half-meter of actual fucking. No problems with the Guild on this one.

The wind picked up, and the smell of rain reached Dirisha as they neared the entrance to Kivu's. Colin here would keep the shippers off her back, she could drink and eat in cool comfort, while the rain splattered against the blue tile roof, and the lightning danced on the arrestors. After the storm passed, she could maybe give him a couple of strokes to repay him for the favor; a kiss or two, a quick jack, he'd be happy enough. A good deal for both of them.

The rain began, smacking into the plastcrete in fat drops which spattered like little bombs. The dull gray surface became pocked with darker spots.

Dirisha pulled at Colin's arm. "Come on, Deuce, let's get inside!"

The cool air of the interior chilled Dirisha, but it felt good after the outside air, which was always body heat or better during the summer. She led Colin toward the back

of the large room which was the shippers' rec-chem center
in Flat Town.

Dirisha was well aware of the looks her body drew as
she moved. She was fifteen, but she was tall and slim, and
her breasts were already larger than her mother's or sister's.
A lot of these men and women wanted her. One of them,
a big brute wearing a freight handler's coverall, stared at
her so hard that Dirisha imagined she could feel his touch.
He sat with his legs spread wide, leaning back in a chair,
drinking splash. When he saw Dirisha's glance, he reached
down between his legs and stroked himself. The bulge there
looked too big to be real; Dirisha hurriedly looked away,
and back at Colin.

To her right, she heard the freight handler laugh. The
sound was coarse, and full of lust. The cold air suddenly
felt too cold, and Dirisha shivered. She knew that kind of
man all too well—she'd learned from her mother and sister
what those men wanted. That one wouldn't be above rape,
and hard rape, at that. Any orifice he wanted—likely all
of them—and fists and feet added in for the fun of it. You
could file a complaint with the Guild or if you were really
stupid, you could call the cools, but it was part of the
business on this world. There were two kinds of people in
a stellar ship's port like Sawa Mji: users and used. Good
timers got paid for it, but they got used, that was the thing.

Dirisha looked back at the freight handler, who continued
to stare at her. She suddenly felt as if her coverlittle covered
nothing; as if the man could see her naked. He grinned.

They reached a table. Dirisha sat first, a mistake. That
put her looking at the freight handler. She pointedly looked
away and at Colin, who was oblivious to all the byplay.

There was no waiter working the floor and the com unit
set into the scarred gray plastic table had long ago ceased
to operate.

"I'll get us something from the bar," Colin said. "What would you like?"

"Splash'll do it," she said. "But no hurry." She didn't want him to leave, for she was sure when he did, the big man eating her with his eyes would move on her. And that thought frightened her. She might be able to downtalk him, but maybe not. If the dork got physical, she couldn't handle that very well, and Colin wouldn't be much help.

"I'll just be a minute," Colin said, as he stood to head for the bar.

Oh, shit.

Dirisha looked around. Six or eight pairs of eyes tried to forge a link with hers, including the handler's. No help from them, things went ugly. A short and smallish woman sat three tables down, snorting spirals of kick-dust; a few local good timers, men and women, cuddled up to clients. Hurry with the drinks, Colin, I'm alone here, really alone—

The freighter handler stood, like some big beast awakening to feed. He padded toward her.

Oh, shit! Colin, come *on*—!

Up close, the man looked gross. He was dirty, his coverall stained with synlube and grime; he needed a depil wash and his breath stank. He leaned over almost to the point of touching Dirisha before he spoke.

"What say we go someplace, dish? I got something special for you, a *big* surprise, you copy? Big."

Dirisha shook her head, afraid. "I'm with somebody." She nodded toward the bar.

Brute didn't bother to look toward the bar. "Kiddie brass won't fuss. He's uplevels, he's not gonna make ripples over the likes of you 'n' me. Come on."

Dirisha felt her mouth go dry as the fear climbed higher in her. "N–no. I can't."

"Am I gonna hafta tenderize you some, dish? I like it

tender." He flexed the fingers of one big hand into a fist and held it under Dirisha's chin.

Dirisha rode the edge of panic. He could hurt her, maybe real bad, before anybody could pull him off—assuming anybody wanted to bother trying. Dirisha swallowed dryness, and shook her head. "No. I'll go with you." She was so frightened she wanted to throw up, to pee, to scream and run. Maybe if she took good care of him, got him off fast and hard, he wouldn't beat her. That hope fell as she saw him grin and felt his fingers clamp onto her arm tightly enough to bruise.

"What's happening here?"

Colin! Dirisha felt a rush of relief. Colin would get pounded if he tried to stop Brute, she was sure of that, but maybe she could get away while it was happening. But probably Colin wouldn't be stupid—

"Bend off," Brute said. "Me 'n' dark meat here have business, isn't that right, dish?"

Dirisha knew her eyes were wide, and she shook her head. "No, I—" Brute squeezed her arm so hard, Dirisha gasped. "Ah!"

Colin reached out and laid his hand on Brute's shoulder. "Let her go!"

The move was fast and savage: Brute released Dirisha and slammed his fist into Colin's belly; the younger man bent suddenly, trying to breathe, and before he could straighten, the freight handler clubbed downward with one thick forearm, catching Colin across the shoulders. The move flattened Colin onto the dirty floor.

Dirisha tried to bolt, but Brute was faster. He blocked her path, arms stretched wide, grinning.

Dirisha spun, looking for an exit. There was no place to go.

The small woman who had been noselining kick-dust looked at Dirisha. The amphetaminic gleamed from the woman's eyes as she took in the scene. For a moment, Dirisha locked gazes with the woman, in a wordless plea for help.

"C'mon, dish. Time to go make me feel good."

Dirisha turned, and Brute grabbed at her. She lunged away, pulling her arms to her chest.

"I said now, meat!"

"Back out, friend," came a quiet voice from behind Dirisha. The girl turned, and saw the woman standing there, legs wide, arms held up, and her fingers spread into claws.

The freight handler laughed. "Back out? Shit, I might— but with two dishes instead of one!" Brute grinned, but the grin faded as the small woman caught and held his gaze with her own. She looked... insolent, that was the word which came to Dirisha's mind. Not the least bit afraid.

Brute's grin faded. "Bend off, cunt. This don't concern you."

"Yes, it does," the woman said. "Let her go and back out."

Behind the bar, the tender was coding in a call for the cools, but they wouldn't get here in time, Dirisha knew. She found herself holding her breath.

The freight handler glanced around. Everyone was watching him, and Dirisha saw him set his teeth; muscles jumped in his face. "Remember, you asked for it," he said. He stepped toward the small woman, more swagger than anything else. His grin returned.

Brute's smile vanished as if slapped from his face. His mouth gaped and he groaned. It happened so fast, Dirisha wasn't sure of what she had seen, but what it looked like was the little woman snapped her foot up and kicked Brute square between the legs. The noise of her foot smacking into his groin was loud in the silent pub.

While the surprise still danced over his face, the little woman moved again.

Once, when she'd been very young, Dirisha had gone to the offworld fauna exhibit at the Flat Town Fair. There had been a lizard there, from some far world, a reddish creature no bigger than her hand, as harmless looking as could be. While she watched, one of the zookeepers dropped a grain rat into the pen. The rat was a big one, almost three times the size of the poor lizard, and Dirisha gasped, afraid for the reptile. She had once seen a big dog driven off by a pair of such rats, an alley mutt hungry enough to attack a human child. The lizard was as good as dead.

The rat spied the lizard and set to pounce; before he could, the lizard darted in, took a hunk of skin and flesh the size of a man's thumb out of the rat's throat, and was half a meter away before the rat realized he was hurt. Three times more the lizard whipped in and out, scoring deeply on the rat, before the stunned mammal fell over and died. Dirisha had been amazed, as had most of the other watchers.

Now, ten years later, Dirisha watched this woman take out the freight handler, much as the lizard had taken the rat. Her hands and elbows slammed into the man's face and neck; her knees thudded into his crotch; her booted feet lanced across his legs and ankles. Brute tried to back away, but the woman stayed with him, pounding continuously. She was the lizard and he was the rat, and he never had a chance, for all his size and strength. It seemed like a long time, but Dirisha later reckoned it at about ten seconds. When Brute fell, it was like a refuse chute blown down by a lightning bolt. He hit the floor hard enough to shake Dirisha, and he did not move to rise.

The woman stood next to the fallen man for a moment, her legs splayed in a funny-looking squat, her arms and hands held rigid. Then she relaxed and straightened. Her face was serious. She turned to look at Dirisha.

"Th–thank you," Dirisha began. "That was–was—"

"—nothing, girl. Don't you have any self-respect? Why are you here? Didn't he have the price?"

"No, you're wrong, I wasn't good-timing—"

"No? But you have, haven't you? And you will again. I know you, I've seen you on a dozen worlds. I don't know why I bothered." She turned, to leave the pub.

"Wait!" Dirisha called. "I–I want to—I need to . . ." she stopped. What, Dirisha? What do you want to say? She's right, isn't she?

No!

Yes.

As she watched the small woman exit, Dirisha had a moment of clarity, a vision of what her life would be like: she would meet this man in one of his many forms, and paid or not, he would use her, as he had been about to do. Who would save her, then? Would she grow used to it, like her older sister and mother had done? Learn to pop dorph for the pain when one of the dink-dorks abused her? File routine complaints with the Guild, like the others did? Would she elect to have four or five children, to help pay the overhead, like her mother did? Carefully ease them into the business, to give herself a rest after ten or twenty years of selling herself to anybody with the price?

Yes, that was what she could do. That was all she could do, she was unprepared for anything else. What she had been looking forward to a few minutes ago now seemed a finite and futile line straight to the final chill. She was fifteen, she saw the end of the ride, and it was unbearably ugly.

Unbearably ugly.

No! She would get out! Get offworld, learn something else—!

What? How?

Dirisha looked at the fallen forms of the two men, Brute

and Colin. The younger man was as a child, she knew, he could be . . . handled. There had to be a way.

There had to be a way.

NINE

DIRISHA LAY ON her back on the bed, staring at the ceiling. Geneva lay next to her, propped on one elbow, gently rubbing the older woman's flat stomach.

"What happened then?" the blonde asked quietly.

Dirisha blinked, turned slightly to look at the woman who loved her, and sighed. "What happened? I helped Colin up from the rec-chem pub's floor, brushed him off, then took him to a cheap quick-crib and seduced him. I was his third woman, I think, and certainly his best. I made sure of that. His ship was berthed for a month; I had that long to get from him what I had to have: knowledge. I traded my fifteen year-old body for as much as I could get him to teach me. He duped a disk from his ship—the *Go Placid*, I'll never forget the freighter's logo, it lit every time the holoproj accessed the damned program—and that's where

I got my secondary education, from that disk. Colin helped me set it up, he helped me start learning it, but it took two years of real-time before I could self-test a ninety percent on it. Colin was long gone, of course, but he'd been well-paid for his efforts. And by seventeen, I had a little more knowledge about the galaxy."

"What were you doing for . . . I mean, how did you . . . manage?"

"To survive? I joined the Guild. Became a good-timer. But I knew it was only temporary. When I turned seventeen, I left the Guild and got a job—room and board and classes— in a local dojo. I started the study of Oppugnate, my first Art. I didn't have any money, I busted my butt, but I wasn't sexing boozed or stoned shippers. I was learning a skill which would buy my way out, I used it right. I knew it could be done—that woman who had saved me from the freight handler had done it, so I could do it. I was young, healthy and willing to do anything it took."

Dirisha fell silent, lost again in her memories.

TEN ─────────────────────────

MWALIMU SLAPPED HER across the face with the back of his hand. Dirisha's head twisted, but she didn't cry out. It was a contemptuous strike, it stung, but there was more noise associated with it than pain; more shame than sound or hurt.

"Stupid!" Mwalimu said. "You have fecalimo for brains! You move like a cow!"

Dirisha nodded. "Yes, Instru'isto." She agreed, but she did not say she was sorry—one never said that to Instru'isto.

The big man turned away, to the rest of the class. The dojo was cramped with twenty students in it, even though they all sat *seiza*, hip-to-hip. The plastic straw mats were worn and frayed, with a decade of ground-in dirt Dirisha could never get out, no matter how hard she scrubbed. The cheap plastic mirrors were age-warped and scratched, from the uncounted impacts of staves, knives and bodies. The room was nearly as hot as outside, and sweat rolled from the faces of the students into their dirty-gray thinskins, staining the material dark where it touched.

"You see how clumsily she performed her technique! I was stopped, but her form was execrable. She might have knocked me cold, had she been set correctly. Never do it as you have seen her do it!"

Instru'isto Mwalimu turned away and stalked toward his office, a man thoroughly disgusted with the world.

Dirisha saw two of the students smile at her, but she kept her face as expressionless as she could. Instru'isto would sometimes—

Mwalimu spun on the balls of his feet suddenly, eyes wide. The grinning students tried to clear their faces, but it was too late. Mwalimu raised from his crouch and smiled, showing a broken front tooth he hadn't had time to have fixed yet. "Ah, Haleem and Mahimbo—you find something amusing?"

"No, Instru'isto—!"

"Shut up! You find something amusing."

The two men looked stricken. "Y-yes, Instru'isto," they said, in unison.

"Good. You will therefore amuse the rest of this class of buffoons. Up, and freestyle." Mwalimu's smile grew wider. "Blood and bones, you-who-are-amused."

The nineteen year-old Dirisha suppressed an urge to swallow dryly. Blood and bones meant just that: they would spar until someone drew blood— or a bone was broken.

One did not smile in Instru'isto Mwalimu's advanced Oppugnate class. Ever.

If Instru'isto was gone, a B&B session would usually end quickly: one student or another would offer a clean shot to the nose or mouth, it would be taken lightly, and blood would flow, ending the fight. But Instru'isto showed no signs of leaving, and trying to avoid pain while he watched was worth a sparring session with *him,* and there was nothing worse. 'Brutal' took on new meanings when Instru'isto made you dance with him.

The two men wore green pins on their thinskins, they had some skill and were both very strong. They bowed, and started.

It took five minutes before a sidekick from Haleem smacked into Mahimbo's rib cage. Everyone heard the wet snap as Mahimbo was thrust back two meters. He did not drop his hands and clutch at his side, though. He merely nodded briefly, and shuffled back toward his opponent. If Dirisha had not heard the rib go, Mahimbo's face would not have told her of his injury.

"Enough," Instru'isto said. He waved his hand lazily. "Sit down." He turned back toward Dirisha, who still stood in a wide-legged riding horse stance in front of the class. "Take them through the Nine Postures. Then work the heavy bag for twenty minutes. See that Mahimbo's rib is ortho-bonded—*after* he works the bag."

Dirisha nodded. "Yes, Instru'isto!"

The man turned his back and stalked into his office.

Dirisha waited until he was out of sight, then nodded toward the class. She felt sorry for Mahimbo, but not sorry enough to allow him to shirk his workout. She'd had six of her ribs broken, four on the left, two on the right, and she knew what it was like to finish a workout in pain.

"First Posture," she said.

Obediently, the students jumped to their feet, to practice the single-step attack-and-defense. They moved as if Instru'isto Himself was watching—as well he might be, through the one-way plastic mirror set in his office wall. Blood and bones might toughen one in the end, but in the short run, it was painful.

* * *

It was the last eve of Agosti, her twentieth birthday, and it had been a long day for Dirisha. Beginning at dawn, for three hours, she had worked around the dojo, cleaning the showers, scrubbing the mats, dusting and wiping all of the weapons in Mwalimu's collection, as well as cleaning his office. Sometimes, he slept in the office, and the place was always a wreck after he left. Nobody knew where Instru'isto lived; he vanished after classes, mostly, and if he had a home or family, no one in the dojo knew of either.

After cleaning up, and a quick breakfast of multigrain bread and cheese, with some vegetable juice, Dirisha had ten minutes to warm up before the first beginner's class started. She was responsible for teaching four of these, ninety minute sessions, before a break for midday. She then had an hour to practice her forms and postures on her own, before Instru'isto led the first advanced class. There were two daily, and she was expected to attend them both. After the last advanced class, Dirisha spent some time working out with a couple of the other brown pins, freestyle and weapon work. Supper came just before the evening clean up; then she was free. Sometimes, she clicked a ball into her reader and studied; sometimes, she went for a walk in the muggy air; often, she simply fell into an exhausted sleep, early.

On this particular day, she had just finished working the long spear, and was going to lock the back portal when Instru'isto appeared from his office. They were alone in the dojo.

"I hope you aren't too tired," he said.

Dirisha looked at him, puzzled.

"Because," he continued, "it's time you took the black pin test. Tonight. Now."

Dirisha sucked in a quick breath. "What?"

Instru'isto grinned. "Let me guess: you had thought to

work up to it gradually, take it on a day when you were fresh and rested, with a cheering throng of your fellow students to help you along, right?"

Dirisha stood mute. Well, yes, those were some of the things she had planned upon—

Intsru'isto interrupted her thoughts. "The technical difference between a brown pin and a black pin is very slight— you will hardly know any more the day after the test than the day before, should you pass it. The difference is in attitude, in spirit. I have never given the black pin lightly— five times in fifteen years—and without the attitude of which I speak, such rank is impossible to obtain."

Dirisha was frightened; as much as anything, Instru'isto's speech scared her. She had never heard him speak in such a . . . cultured manner. Always, the man had been spare, almost gruff, and the cadence of his language now seemed unreal. Where did he go when he left here? What was he, when he wasn't Instru'isto, Fifth Degree Oppugnate black pin?

"So, Dirisha, the two of us begin a dance. You will perform everything you have learned for me—all the forms, each technique. If you do them perfectly, then we shall dance together, you and I, blood and bones. At the end, you shall have become a black pin or you shall have need of a vat of orthobondic and medical care. Lock the doors."

It took nearly three hours for her to run through all her katas and defensive tactics. Dirisha demonstrated basic blocks and strikes, which by this time were second nature; she also cut the warm, damp air with a variety of ancient weaponry: flails, knives, spears, swords, staves. She passed the point of exhaustion and came into a second wind toward the end, but she was not sure how well she was moving. It *felt* okay, but what did it look like?

When she was done, her thinskin was drenched in sweat, none of it left dry. She felt as if she had stood under a hot saltwater shower.

Instru'isto nodded. He bowed, watching her carefully, then slid into a fighting stance, hands raised to cover his face and groin.

Dirisha mirrored her instructor's stance, her own hands automatically finding the defensive pattern.

They stood three meters apart, watching each other, not speaking. That he would hurt her, she doubted not at all. The black pin meant nothing, now: survival occupied her thoughts.

Instru'isto slid forward a few centimeters. He was centered, taut, and Dirisha had never seen him look so dangerous. She tried to breathe evenly, but her air came in smaller portions than she wished.

The big man slid closer.

Dirisha held her ground, waiting.

He moved, whipping forward with a snap kick for her knee—

—Dirisha V-stepped to her left and brought her own right foot up in a spring kick for his solar plexus—

—He spun away from it and helicoptered his fist at her temple—

—She ducked and thrust at his eyes with her stiffened fingers—

—He slammed an elbow at her throat—

—Dirisha began to leap away, then stopped. It was what he had taught her to do, and he would know it. She stopped, and fired a flat punch, putting her shoulder into it, twisting her hip for added power. There was in the movement, a moment of clarity, when she *knew* the technique would work. Time stretched, like hot plastic, but the move was only the work of a half-second—

Even so, Instru'isto twisted and almost avoided the punch,

so great was his skill. Almost.

The two striking knuckles of Dirisha's compacted sun-fist caught Instru'isto just above the left eye: the skin tore as the man's head snapped back; a trickle of blood flowed through the brow and along the socket of his eye.

Instru'isto slid back, and bowed, deeper than Dirisha had ever seen him do so. When he straightened, he was grinning. He unpinned the black badge from his thinskin and tossed it at Dirisha, who caught it in shocked awe.

"Welcome to the club, Dirisha."

The man was grossly fat and wore four shades of rouge, looking like a good-timer himself. He was not; he was a jewel merchant from Mti, sister world to Dirisha's planet, the only other habitable globe in the Ndama System. He sat at a fancy table in the Restaurant Danelle, stuffing his gut with expensive candied fruit. A parasite, Dirisha thought, soft and contemptible. He was her target, however, and what he was was not so important as who he was: a pass offworld—if she played it right.

The merchant's bodyguard saw her as she walked toward their table. He was a big man, the bodyguard, replete with muscle mass and a face which had known many fists from many angles. Instru'isto had seen him work, though, and Dirisha knew the man depended on power and not skill. It was risk, but all of life was risk.

"Whadda ya want?" the hulk said.

"I'll talk to your master, cur."

"Ya don't pass here." Hulk raised one heavy hand to shove against Dirisha's chest. "I hear it first."

The fat jewel dealer looked up from his meal, mildly interested, no more. Some orange concoction was smeared over his lips, and his eyes were drug-glazed within their layers of fat.

Dirisha caught the outstretched hand and twisted. Chang,

but the man was strong! Even with the leverage and her quickness, the arm barely moved. Well. There were ways.

Dirisha pivoted under the thick arm and drove her elbow into Hulk's solar plexus. The muscle was solid there, too, but the force of her strike relaxed the arm she still held a bit. Enough. Dirisha twisted the arm and turned her body at the same time. Despite his strength, the bodyguard went down, grunting.

The merchant woke up, eyes wide. Dirisha figured he had good reason to fear thieves; perhaps even assassins. He looked around, but there was no place to flee without passing Dirisha. He stared at his protector.

The bodyguard was locked, he wasn't going anywhere. Dirisha could break his arm or knock him senseless now, as she chose. She smiled at the merchant.

"Wh-what do ye want?"

"A job," Dirisha said.

"D-doing what?"

"Bodyguarding."

"I have such." He nodded at Hulk.

"Not doing so good, is he Deuce? You should let me replace him."

The merchant looked at the dark-skinned woman, then at the muscular man she held helpless. The fat man smiled, and Dirisha knew she wouldn't spend another week on the planet for which she was named. Her smile far surpassed that of her new employer.

She was on her way. Where wasn't important, only that it was somewhere—she had a galaxy to choose from.

ELEVEN

GENEVA'S HAND LAY unmoving on Dirisha's stomach. The blonde said, "How hard it was for you."

Dirisha nodded. "It made me hard, too, hon. As soon as we hit Mti, I dropped the merchant and got a job bouncing in a pub. I joined the Atemi Waza Gymnasium—Mwalimu suggested I learn a wrestling art, to complement his boxing style. Atemi works against the joints, involves a lot of throws and tumbling. I stayed there two years.

"Still on Mti, I studied Kinzoku—that's metal work, mostly throwing darts and knives—and that took another three years. From there, I spaced to Greaves, and learned to play Mkono-sio Haki—Illegal Hands—another striking style. I picked up stuff here and there along the way, informally. And I began to play the Flex."

"The Musashi Flex," Geneva said. "Red walked that path for a time. And Khadaji once fought in a tourney."

Dirisha took a deep breath, allowed it to escape, then looked at Geneva. "I liked it a lot, at first. The competition, the wonder—can I beat this guy? Will he do me, instead?—and I played it hard, too. I won, I lost sometimes. There are people walking the Flex who could give Pen a hard time, Geneva, totally dedicated to the game. I wanted to find something beyond what I was, but I never did. After a time, I began to wonder if I would ever be more than just an aging player, a ronin who'd eventually get taken out by some kid on some backwater world, as if I'd never been."

"Is that why you're here?"

Dirisha thought about it for a few seconds before she spoke. "Partially, I suppose. Another part of me wants to learn from you and Pen and take the new Art back out on the circuit. Part of me doesn't know what I want, it just wants to rest and not have to think."

The two women lay quietly for a time; then, Geneva leaned over and softly kissed Dirisha's cheek. "It doesn't matter, you know."

"Geneva, I've killed more than a dozen people in personal combat. I've probably sent three times that many to full medical-construct, so badly were they damaged. And I've hurt hundreds in the last ten years. There was a time when I liked it, Geneva. Even the killing."

"But not any more?"

"No. Not any more."

"It doesn't matter. I still love you."

Dirisha rolled over onto her side and faced Geneva. The blonde was smiling tenderly, and Dirisha wanted nothing so much as to be able to say those same words to her, in truth. But she couldn't, she was wrapped too tightly in what she had been, what she had done. Instead, she hugged Geneva to her, and they stayed that way, breast to breast, for a long time.

It was the best she could do, all things considered.

* * *

Dirisha came around the corner of the corridor leading to the dining hall, and saw Red about to shoot Geneva in the back. Almost without thinking, Dirisha raised her own spetsdöd and took in a breath to call out a warning to the other woman. Two against one, but there were no rules against that.

Dirisha needn't have bothered. Even as Red fired, his daughter dropped flat, so that the blunt dart sang over her head; she rolled onto her back and thrust both her weapons toward her father. The sound of two spetsdöds on full-auto filled the corridor. Red's hands jumped, from the impact of Geneva's flechettes, and his own return fire went wide. His time ran out for the mutual kill—and Geneva won.

Several students peeped from around doorways at the scene, and their voices were muted when they spoke.

"—see *that*? She got Red—!"

"—never saw anybody move so fast—!"

"—sweet Buddha, how can anybody shoot like that—?"

Red's hands had angry red splotches on them where half a dozen small missiles had stung them, but he was smiling as Geneva got to her feet. He walked to his daughter and put one arm around her shoulders. "Way to go, kid."

As they walked off together down the corridor, Red glanced back at Dirisha. There seemed to be tears in the man's eyes, and Dirisha was certain those tears were not from any pain he might have felt. He was one of the best, he had just been beaten by one of his students, and that might make him sad; on the other hand, it was his daughter who had taken him, and that must mean something else altogether.

"He's happy," came a voice from behind Dirisha. Pen. Even if she hadn't recognized it, nobody else could sneak up on her the way Pen always seemed to be able to do.

Dirisha looked at the shrouded figure.

"She's better than she's ever been before," Pen said. "And she was already the best."

Dirisha nodded. "I know."

"Do you know why?"

Dirisha shook her head.

Pen looked down the corridor. "Want to take a walk?"

"Sure."

She followed Pen outside. He began to lead her across the artificial plateau, toward a section of scrub wood a kilometer away from the school. It was cooler these last few days, as the tilt and orbit of Renault brought autumn to the hemisphere. The vegetation around Simplex-by-the-Sea had begun to go to the warm colors: reds, yellows, browns, all dotted the stunted trees and bushes now, amidst the green.

"Geneva has always been something special," Pen said. "But lately, she's become more than ever before."

Dirisha said nothing.

"She's going to be put in a position of real importance when she leaves here. She could be the cog that turns the big wheel at just the right moment."

The scrub trees loomed.

"In fact," Pen said, "any of the students could be that cog."

Dirisha reached the first of the trees. She touched the rough bark with the fingertips of one hand. The tree felt hot, a surprise. "Some of us are less likely to do that than others."

Pen drew next to Dirisha. He looked properly inscrutable within the gray folds of his robe. His eyes looked all-too-wise, though. "Meaning yourself?"

Dirisha picked a fleck of bark from the tree, examined it, then tossed it away. She returned her attention to Pen. She shrugged.

Pen turned to stare back at the school. "You know any-thing about integratics?"

"Some kind of theoretical sociobiology, isn't it?"

"More than theoretical," Pen said. "It's very practical. The Siblings of the Shroud have been working with it for some years. In a limited way, of course." He looked away from the school and back at Dirisha. "The students here, for instance, have been chosen not only for their abilities as individuals, but also for how they will mesh with the others here. We have secured in-depth psychological profiles on each student—and each instructor. If someone is going to hate someone else, we want to know it."

Dirisha carried the statement a step farther. "And if some-body is likely to . . . love somebody, you want to know that, too, right?"

Pen chuckled. "One of the things I like about talking with you is that there is never the need to belabor the ob-vious. Yes, we want to know that, too."

"So you had a pretty good idea that Geneva would find herself attracted to me."

"I am surprised it took so long."

"And the purpose of this little manipulation?"

"You already know. Since you arrived, Geneva has be-come more . . . complete. She has transcended her self—she now loves, in a way she has not loved before. Before, she only had an image, that of Khadaji, the myth. Now, she has the reality—you."

Dirisha rubbed one hand up and down against the tree. The coarse bark felt good against her palm. "I like Geneva," she said. "I feel more comfortable with her than I've felt with anybody in a long time. She's a good kid, sweet, but—"

"But you don't love her," Pen finished.

"I don't. I wish I could."

"It doesn't matter. It's enough that she loves you."

"That's what she said. I don't see it."

"You will, someday." His smile wrinkles appeared. "You might want to have a talk with Mayli Wu, when you get some time."

Dirisha felt uncomfortable about this whole conversation; as if there was some kind of threat she could not see, but could feel. She decided to change the subject. "Is it true that Sister—Mayli used to be a medic?"

"Board-certified in urology," Pen said.

"Why'd she give that up to be a prostitute?"

"She discovered what love was. Call it field work."

"That's a little flip."

"It's the truth. Ask her."

"I will."

Pen stood silently for a moment, and Dirisha began to wonder just what this hike was meant to impart. She tried to cast it into fugue-mode, but it seemed to be more twisty than she could unravel. From her dealings with Pen so far, she knew he never did anything without a reason. What was he getting ready to drop onto her?

To her surprise, Pen said, "Well. Thanks for the walk. I'll see you at the school." And he started back.

For an instant, Dirisha had an urge to point her finger at his back and blast him with her spetsdöd. But even as she thought it, Pen cleared his right hand from the robe, to show his own weapon.

Damn! Was he telepathic? He *knew* she wanted to do it! And just what was this all about?

A small thought bounced up and down in a far corner of Dirisha's mind, trying to get her attention. When she finally noticed it, the thought suddenly grew to fill her consciousness with its simple truth: remember Heisenberg, kiddo. If you are an effect, and affecting someone like Geneva, you too are part of this integratic dance. You can see what you are doing—can you also see what is being done? To *you?*

Once again, Dirisha resolved to be aware. The incident on the ferry, and the love Geneva now felt for her were intended, she knew that.

What else did Pen have planned for her?

As she watched Pen, now a hundred meters away, Dirisha felt an old memory suddenly come alive. Something in this situation sparked it, some similarity. It shouldn't, that incident was nothing like this one, but there it was. She watched Pen's figure in the distance, remembering. . . .

Dirisha watched the figure in the distance, and wondered how she'd been so stupid as to come to this place. Vul was the second moon of Kalk, in the Svare System, a barren, arid place kept alive only by the Tarp which formed a clear dome over the settlement. A big moon, to be sure, enough to give a person four-fifths of a gee—and a headache from the local sun, if that person forgot her droptac filters. It was a pit of a place, there was no reason for anybody not born here to come and visit—and no reason for anybody to *be* born here, that Dirisha could see. So why was she standing out in the ankle-deep orange dust, watching the solitary figure approach?

She grinned. The Flex sent a person to some odd places, Deuce, sure enough. Even to this pit. She'd heard from an instructor on Kalk that there was a fighter here, a woman who either had been a player who'd retired, or still was a player who was hiding out, or who ate rocks and pissed gravel just for the fun of it. The Flex was full of half-truths and rumors, and if only one in a hundred were true, then there were men who could breathe vac, defeat a hundred at a kick, or become invisible with a snap of two fingers. This much was certain: the locals knew who Dirisha was looking for, and they spoke of this player-not-player with great respect.

After five years in the game, Dirisha was not so easily

impressed. She'd lost a few, but won a lot more; she had taken six to the end, and out of it; she knew she was good.

The figure drew nearer, not growing all that much. A smallish woman, though that meant little. Dirisha's first bad loss had been to a man not much bigger than a child. She'd underestimated his skill and strength, and he'd beaten her bloody and senseless for her lapse.

She knew better, now.

The woman was centered well, despite the gravity and the dust. Dirisha had practiced moving in the lower gee for a week before she'd gone looking for the locals' champion. Anything less would have been stupid.

The woman was close enough for Dirisha to see her face. Oddly, she seemed familiar, though Dirisha couldn't place her. She knew a lot of the major players, but this woman wasn't from those memories.

Dirisha saw the woman recognize her for what she was, and she smiled, teeth bright against her dark skin.

The small woman was dressed in a dustwrap suit, sealed at the neck, ankles and wrists, and she stopped three meters away.

"What say, Sister?" Dirisha felt tight, wired, ready to spring.

The woman sighed. "I thought somebody like you might come. I was hoping to avoid having to hurt anybody here, but if you're determined, I'm ready to show you the way." A deliberate pause. "Sister."

The voice did it. The face might not have given it to her, but the voice brought it back: Dirisha remembered the woman, knew where she had seen her before. Her surprise must have overcome her control, for the woman smiled.

"What's the matter, Sister? See a ghost?"

Dirisha smiled, she couldn't help it. "Lizard!"

"I didn't copy that, Sister. Say again."

Dirisha shook her head. "You wouldn't understand the

term, it's personal. But I know you—you were on Dirisha, about ten standards ago. In Flat Town."

"So?" The woman edged forward a hair, setting her feet more firmly on the chalk-like ground under the orange dust. She turned slightly to one side, to present a smaller target.

"You took out a freight handler in Kivu's, a guy hard-timing a young woman." *A child*, Dirisha thought.

"I lost count of the pub-scrubs I've shaken up, Sister. A long time ago." She slid a few centimeters closer.

Automatically, Dirisha moved her own stance backward a hair. Then she stopped, and forced herself to relax. "I saw it. I was the girl. You saved my ass."

"I can't even remember it, night-face. It was nothing."

Dirisha shook her head again. "It was something. It refocused my life."

The small woman laughed. "You became a player? Walking the fucking Flex? Shit. What were you before?"

"A trull. A good-timer."

"Not much improvement. Some, but not much." She moved in a little closer, her hands starting to come up.

"Don't," Dirisha said. "I can't fight you. You gave me a way out. I worked for years to be like you, as good as you."

"Well, now's your chance to find out if you made it, little sister. Or, maybe 'daughter' might be better, hey?"

"Look, I don't want to do this. Forget I was ever here."

"How can I? You brought all that fucking history with you. I was one of the best when you were still a kid. I still am."

Dirisha nodded. "I'm not arguing."

"But do you believe, night-face? That I was better than you then, and I'm better than you now?"

Pride rose in Dirisha, ego-fed and fat. "You were better, then. Not now. I know how good you were, I studied your moves in memory a thousand times. But—"

"But I'm old and slow and you're young and fast, right?"

Anger flared. She was trying to give the woman a way out—why wouldn't she take it?

"Is that right, good-timer-who-thinks-she-can-play-with-the-best?"

Dirisha dropped her center, and took a deep breath. "Yes. That's right!"

The woman lunged—

Fifteen seconds later, the woman who had once saved Dirisha's life was unconscious. Not dead, not even badly injured, that's how much better Dirisha was than she.

Dirisha hadn't been able to understand the fight, then.

Dirisha Zuri—it meant "window to beauty" in her native language—stood staring at Matador Villa. The memory of the fight against her one-time benefactor still pained her whenever she recalled it. She'd understood why the woman had to try her, but only later, after she had begun to tire of the Flex. She understood other things, too. If she had only been a little wiser, she could have backed down, and given her youthful idol face, honor. She could have even fought and lost—pretended to lose—it wouldn't have cost her any more pain than some of her early sparring sessions with Instru'isto. But she hadn't been wise, she'd been young and stupid and full of herself. So she had taken the older woman, had beaten her in such a way that there could be no doubts about who was the better fighter. It had been a sin to do that, Dirisha knew that now. Hindsight, and useless, but she at least knew. Now.

What hindsight would she be viewing in a year or five years or twenty years—assuming she was still alive? Had she really gotten any wiser? Or was she just fooling herself?

Dirisha stared at the school, and leaned back against the scrub tree. She was more troubled than she could ever recall being. Damn. . . .

TWELVE

TALVO SEN, SUPREME High President and Beloved Ruler for Life of the Glorious Corporate State of Mzaha, smiled nervously into the photomutable gel of the broadcast camera's eye. Many of his eight million subjects would be watching the cast, and he obviously wanted to impress them.

Dirisha was not impressed. President Sen was a man she cared not at all about, save that he was in her charge. All that mattered was that he survive the holoprojic cast—a thing ordinarily not something one would worry about, since appearing on an audiovisual net was seldom fatal, in and of itself. But somebody wanted to assassinate Sen, and Dirisha's job was to prevent such an assassination.

Dirisha stood to the President's left, wearing a set of soft gray flexweave orthoskins and her spetsdöds, watching the technicians flurry around the broadcast gear as the time for

the program drew near. The room was large—President Sen
could hardly occupy a less-than imposing office—a good
eight meters square, and even the four technicians and all
their equipment did little to shrink the space. There were
no windows, and only two doors. The main entrance was
ringed with detection gear—axial scanners, HO detectors
and a zap field—and the emergency exit was a one-way
that could only be unlocked from the inside by President
Sen's right palm print. The floor and ceiling were both
ferrofoam, and laced with sensors. Dirisha had inspected
each tech as he or she entered, done a physical and hard-
object scan, and a spec-chrome for possible contact poisons.
The four techs were all clean. When she had learned of the
broadcast, Dirisha had taken a quick-course in broadcast
engineering. When she checked each piece of equipment
allowed into the room, she knew what it was she was checking, and what it should look like. In theory, it would be
almost impossible for anybody dangerously armed to get
into this room, short of an all-out attack with heavy weapons. Dirisha had a couple of armored monitors set outside,
to cover the building, so if somebody *did* throw heavy stuff
at it, she'd get enough warning to hustle Sen into the emergency exit.

She had it covered, she figured.

One of the techs dropped a lens mount. The expensive
piece of equipment thumped down on the thick carpet and
bounced. They were a clumsy bunch. That was the second
time somebody had mishandled the cast gear.

Another tech said, "One minute, President Sen."

The ruler leaned over and put the palms of his hands flat
on his desk, and did a sort of half-push up. It was a gesture
he sometimes did when nervous.

Well he should be nervous, Dirisha thought. He was not
a popular man. Three times in the past week, people had
tried to send President Sen to join his ancestors. Three times,

Dirisha had kept him alive. A fanatic with a hand wand had tried to get Sen from a crowd; a woman cook had tried to poison the President; a religious cabal had sent a team of assassins with bombs against the ruler of Mzaha. Dirisha had stopped them all. So far.

"Thirty seconds." The tech calling time looked into his viewer. "Cats' blood, Rimo, the posterior illuminator is in the frame. Get over there and move it, stat!"

The named tech scurried to move the offending light. Dirisha watched him circle behind the President, her spetsdöd held ready to shoot if the man moved a hair toward Sen. Instead, the tech got one foot tangled in the base of the illuminator as he tried to move the light, and fell. He almost went headlong, but managed to save himself from falling by slamming into the emergency exit. Ouch. The tech shoved away from the door.

"Come on, Rimo! We're at ten seconds!"

Rimo grinned with embarrassment and tugged at the illuminator.

"Okay, okay, now move out of the frame!"

Rimo scampered back behind the holoproj camera.

Dirisha looked at the tech directing.

"Seven, six, five, four, three, two, one—go!"

President Sen smiled, and as he did, one of the technicians behind the camera suddenly pulled a strip of metal away from the camera's base and screamed. "Death to dictators!" Then the woman lunged forward.

Before the would-be assassin had moved half a meter, Dirisha shot her, the cough of her spetsdöd loud in the room. What a stupid attack, she never had a chance, why—?

The double cough of a second set of spetsdöds reached Dirisha even as she spun to face the movement she saw peripherally. A gray figure, coming from the emergency exit! President Sen slapped at his cheek where he'd been hit. Before she could bring her spetsdöds around to return

the fire, Dirisha felt the double sting of two more spetsdöd
slugs stitch her belly. Damn! She couldn't even take one of
them with her, for the gray figure danced back into the exit
before she fired! Her darts hissed through the open doorway
harmlessly.

Damn, damn, *damn!* She and Sen were dead—!

Dirisha straightened from her crouch. President Sen lifted
himself off the desk. The suicidal tech with the metal strip
stood and brushed at her slightly-tangled hair.

The gray figure stepped back into the room. Pen.

"I just killed your charge," Pen said, "And you along
with him. How did I do it?"

Dirisha sighed. She thought back over the past few minutes. The clumsy, stumbling techs. The one-way lock.

"Sen's palm print, on the lock."

The tech called Rimo stepped forward and supinated his
right hand. He peeled a thin sheet of plastic away from his
right palm and held it up. Dirisha could see the whorls and
lines on the material. She shook her head.

"You had clues," Pen said.

Dirisha nodded, feeling disgusted. "Sen's habit of push-
ing against his desk top."

"What else?"

"The clumsy techs. That gear is too expensive to let a
hyperspaz play with it. It was a set-up for the lock fall."

"What else?"

"The diversionary attack. There was no way it could have
succeeded—even Sen could have protected himself against
that."

Pen nodded. "Cut it."

The walls of the "President's office" began to fade, as
holoprojic images created by a magnetic-viral computer
dimmed and allowed reality to seep back into the room.
Dirisha and the others—all students or instructors—found
themselves standing in the middle of a large domed struc-

ture, empty save for themselves. Dirisha knew that the other matador students would either be watching her test live, or would see the recording of it later. She sure had screwed it up.

Pen said, "Hindsight is wonderful, but it comes too late. Fortunately, this scenario was only a game. Learn from what you have seen here—no one should make the same mistake Dirisha did. Take nothing for granted." Pen paused. "I'd like to see the assassin."

A door opened and a figure entered the dome.

Dirisha smiled at the approaching woman, and shook her head ruefully. "I should have known," she said.

Geneva didn't smile. "I'm sorry."

"Don't be," Dirisha said. "It's the best thing you could have done for me. It might save my life, someday."

"I know. That's why I did it."

Pen spoke to an unseen audience. "If you want to be able to prevent your charge from such a fate as Dirisha's, you must learn to think like an assassin. If you can conceive of the attack, you can design a defense. In this job, there is no second place winner, second means you lose. Three times, Dirisha kept her charge alive, but she lost him on the fourth. Dead is dead forever. Remember that."

Pen turned and strode away, a dramatic figure in his robes. Most of the others began to follow him.

Dirisha turned to Geneva. "Why didn't you do the shooting? The plan was yours."

"Part of planning is to pick the best people for the job," Geneva said. "Pen was better equipped for that part."

Dirisha cocked her head to one side and smiled at the younger woman. "Really? I think if it came to it, you could outshoot him. I've seen you both work."

"Against somebody else, maybe," Geneva said. She reached out to touch Dirisha's shoulder. "Not against you."

Dirisha felt that stab of feeling again, that uneasy touch

of emotion she'd known since she and Geneva had become close. The woman *loved* her, there was no getting around it. Even though she knew Dirisha didn't feel the same way about her, she still loved her. Damn.

"Well, I'm next in the barrel," Geneva said, breaking the mood. "Probably they'll get me first time."

Geneva was wrong. Nine students tried assassinations against her charge, a portly "industrialist" from Earth. It was only when Pen and Red joined forces that Geneva finally lost; and, even then, she took Red with her, narrowly missing Pen as she went down.

Afterwards, Pen found Dirisha practicing sumito.

"Do you know why we were able to get Geneva's charge?"

"I saw the scenario, she was off-balance by the—"

"No. It was because she didn't really care for him. We do that on purpose, write the charges in as pompous or ignorant or stupid, sometimes. To see if you'll let your personal feelings for a client influence how you do your job. Geneva didn't like him, so she was lax."

"She beat all of us nine times," Dirisha said.

Pen nodded. "Yes. But," he said softly, "if *you* had been her client, she'd still be beating us."

Dirisha stopped her dance. "What's that supposed to mean?"

Pen stood, as inscrutable as always. "It means that what you feel for a client makes a difference. It is difficult under the best of circumstances for a man or woman to be objective—whatever 'objective' is—about anything important. You don't like a client, then your job is just a job, 'objective', nothing more. If you like a client, you work harder for him or her, unconsciously. If you *love* a client and you can still maintain your professional training, *that* client gets everything you have. If you were Geneva's charge, she'd move planets to keep you safe. All the galaxy together would have trouble beating her—love is more powerful than fanaticism. Remember that, Dirisha. It's important."

Pen turned and left, and Dirisha stood watching him. At times, it seemed everything Pen said was ambiguous, full of hidden meanings. Dirisha felt as if she had just heard something profound, only—

She wished she knew what the hell it meant.

THIRTEEN ───────────

DIRISHA WENT TO see Mayli Wu. She found the woman she'd first known as Sister Clamp sitting nude, legs locked in lotus and eyes closed, on a cushion in the meditation chamber. Although Wu was naked, she wore her spetsdöds, and Dirisha felt the other woman's awareness as she slipped into the room. There had been other times when she had known that kind of energy exchange, as another's *ki* flowed and meshed with her own. If she tried to shoot the meditating woman now, Dirisha knew she would be shot at the same instant. That sense of *zanshin* was part of what Flex players craved, part of what the Arts were supposed to give when enlightenment was reached. In all her years of training, Dirisha had known the feeling only a few times, and then only fleetingly. A true Master was supposed to *live* there.

Strange that she should feel it now.

Dirisha sat on her heels, and waited.

After ten minutes, Mayli Wu opened her eyes. She smiled. "Sister. How may I serve you?"

Dirisha said, "I need some answers."

"Of course." Wu unknotted her legs and stretched them in front of herself. She bent at the waist and touched her toes, then straightened. She drew her feet up, knees gaping slightly, and clasped her arms around her legs. "Ask."

"Why did you give up being a medic to become a trull?"

"To learn about love."

Dirisha shook her head. "I was in that business, when I was young. What I learned about was lust, and selfishness."

"You weren't looking in the right direction."

"And you found what you wanted?"

"Yes. I have touched love more than once."

Dirisha digested that. "What is this all about?" She waved her hand, to encompass the whole of Matador Villa. "Really?"

Wu smiled. "Pen has told you."

"You'll pardon me if I say I don't trust Pen any farther than I can fly by flapping my arms. The man is an expert at manipulation, his motives are suspect."

"Everyone's motives are suspect, to you, sister. You don't trust anybody, you never have. It is your greatest strength."

Dirisha nodded. "It's kept me alive."

Wu shook her head. "Your greatest strength, but also your greatest weakness. A flaw in your perfection."

"What are you saying?"

Wu touched the edge of the plastic flesh holding the right spetsdöd to the back of her hand, peeled it up, and dropped the weapon next to her hip. She repeated the process with her other spetsdöd.

Dirisha's breath caught. During the time she'd been here, she'd never seen another student or instructor weaponless. She had gotten so used to seeing everyone armed, the sight of Mayli Wu without her weapons gave her a chill. Now the woman truly looked *naked;* before, she had only been unclothed.

"Why did you do that?"

"Are you going to shoot me? I can't shoot back."

"No. But why did—?" Dirisha stopped, her gaze fixed on Wu's smile. "What makes you think I *won't* shoot? You do think that, don't you?"

"I *know* it."

Dirisha raised one hand and pointed at the center of Wu's chest. "It would only take a flick of my finger to prove you wrong."

"True," the naked woman said. "You *could* do it, easily. But you won't."

Dirisha let her hand fall. She was right. She wouldn't shoot. But how could Wu know?

"How do I know?" Wu said, voicing Dirisha's question. "Because I trust you. Your integrity. Your sense of fairness. Your training. I can see your essence, better than you can see it yourself, and I *know.* In this moment, in this place, I can trust you completely. If someone were to come in here and see me defenseless, another student, they might decide to collect a few easy points by stinging me, but that doesn't worry me, either. Do you know why?"

Dirisha felt herself being swept by emotions, a labile mix of fear, wonder and astonishment. The answer to Wu's question presented itself as though clad in microstacked stainless steel, as solid as a block of compressed lead: *why couldn't anybody who happened by shoot Mayli Wu? Why, because I would protect her from it. Why would I do that? Because she* trusts *me to do it!*

Wu said, "Ah. I see that you understand. A major step. Only one of many you must still take, but a beginning. Even the longest journey must start somewhere."

Shaken, Dirisha could not speak for a moment. Finally, she found her voice. "So Pen told the truth?"

"Certainly. He has not told you everything, but what he says about our purpose is true. You would never have been selected to come here, were you not in accord with it, on some level. The Confed is dying; when it finally collapses, there will be chaos in the ruins. For mankind to rise again at all will be difficult; for people to move in moral directions will be harder still. We can make a difference, if we are properly trained, properly motivated and dedicated. That's what you are learning to do here. But before you can save anybody else, you must learn to save yourself."

Dirisha sat on the edge of her bed, telling the story to Geneva. The two women wore thinskin bodystockings and spetsdöds, no more, and as Dirisha spoke, Geneva came to stand next to the dark-skinned woman.

"She *knew* I wouldn't shoot her," Dirisha said. "There was no doubt, none at all. I don't understand how she could be so *sure*."

Geneva reached out and began to knead at Dirisha's neck, working the tight and hard trapezius with deep pressure of her fingertips. Dirisha hadn't realized how tense she was until she felt the other woman's touch. Bad, that, losing simple muscle control unconsciously. Dirisha took a deep breath, closed her eyes, and relaxed into the massage.

After a moment, the hands stopped. Another moment, and there came the sound of Geneva's spetsdöds thumping onto the bed.

Dirisha opened her eyes and looked up into Geneva's smiling face. The older woman shook her head. "Damn. I'm surrounded by 'em."

Geneva continued the massage, digging harder into the kiatsu points, relaxing the muscles even more. She said, "Is it so hard to believe somebody can trust you?"

"I don't understand the reason why. I could have shot her. I could do the same to you."

"You could. It would be all right if you did."

"You are hopeless."

Geneva's touch lightened, to a gentle stroking motion. "Why? Because I love you? And trust you?"

Dirisha said nothing. That sense of danger which rode her whenever the conversation or her thoughts turned into these channels rode heavily upon her. What was she afraid of?

Geneva slept in Dirisha's bed, exhausted from their love-making, out like a small child. Dirisha sat at her desk, glancing past the holoproj unit at the sleeping figure. She had been floating in this comfortable pond for a long time without really questioning it—one tended not to look at such a gift as this too closely—but now it was time. Along with the skill of sumito, the ability to knock dragonflies from the air with a spetsdöd, Dirisha was getting more than she'd intended. She needed to know more about that. There was information stored in the viral molecular brain of Matador Villa's computer she wanted access to, and she had figured out a way to get it.

The black woman stood and went to her lockbox. Thumbing it open, she withdrew a small holoprojector. She'd bought it from one of the bandit merchants in town, no one at the school knew she had it. Neither did anyone know that Dirisha had spent considerable time in the archives, editing recording spheres which were available to open access. From the lockbox, Dirisha also took a plastic case which held half a dozen vacuum-formed steel marbles. The case was marked, "Galactic Economies in the Modern Age." Five of the balls were, in fact, just that, dull recordings of interest only to a student of economics. The sixth sphere, however, was something else. It was a pass to information held under personal lock—if it worked. It would depend on how sophisticated the computer security system was.

For a moment, she was tempted to use the console here in the room. Geneva was not likely to awaken for anything short of a bomb exploding, at least as long as she knew Dirisha was there. But if she did, Dirisha didn't want to have to explain what she was doing. No, better to do this in privacy.

The hour was late, and although the Villa never shut down completely, it was unlikely Dirisha would run into anybody in the sleeping quarters. She padded down the hall to the small study and entered it. Nobody else was about.

Inside the study, Dirisha locked the door and stroked the computer console into life. The air lit with the Three Rules, as it did every time a remote in-house was used. The words floated holoprojically over the small plastic desk, glowing as though composed of tiny neon tubes.

Quickly, Dirisha set up her projector. She snapped the sphere into the socket, and flicked the unit on. There was a small hum as the projector cycled up. Dirisha touched the "Play" control, and then the "Hold" tab.

The air in front of the computer console shimmered brightly, and the image of Pen appeared, looking somewhat ghostly. Dirisha adjusted a control, and Pen took on more solidity. He seemed almost real, frozen in the middle of a gesture, his mouth open. A holoprojection would not fool anyone with normal human senses this close, but it might fool a computer's remote camera. Dirisha looked at her chronometer. She had timed the recording, and had practiced the sequence several times. She touched the "Hold" control again, counted off three seconds, then stroked the computer console into "Access" mode. She took a deep breath. The computer was designed to hold private files under several command sequences. Material could be locked under simple codes, voice patterns, visual identification, palmprints, or any combination of the four. Most students and instructors just used vocal or visual. If the computer recognized you, it gave you what you wanted, assuming you were cleared for it. It would not give Geneva those files tagged to Dirisha's face, or vice versa. Simple, and usually pretty effective. But recordings could be made, vocally or visually, so there were back-ups.

OPERATING. The word flashed in the air.

The image of Pen spoke. "Personal Files," it said. Those two words had taken Dirisha almost nine hours to find and assemble so they sounded natural. Dirisha started counting. One, two three—

INITIAL IDENTIFICATION SEQUENCE ACCEPTED. VOCAL AND VISUAL. CONFIRMATION REQUIRED.

Dirisha let her breath escape slowly. Here's where it could get tricky. She had made an assumption that Pen would secure his own files as much as possible. So far, so good— The image of Pen leaned toward the holoproj. There was a sensor at the base. As Pen stretched out his right hand, Dirisha leaned in from the side and pressed her own palm against the sensor. It was Pen's palmprint, taken from a cast she had made of it, a thin layer of plastic skin over her own.

SECONDARY IDENTIFICATION ACKNOWLEDGED, the computer flashed. AWAITING OPERATIVE CODE SEQUENCE.

The image of Pen stood unspeaking. Dirisha realized her timing was a little slow. Would the computer see that as a problem? Was there a limit on how long it would wait?

"Khadaji," The image said.

Dirisha held her breath again. She reached for the "Hold" control on the projector. It was pure guesswork, using Khadaji's name. The recording had three more words it could try, in case that one didn't work. If the computer queried a wrong command, the image of Pen would say, "A mistake. Cancel that, the code is 'Matador.'" If that didn't work, there was "Sumito" and "spetsdöd" in reserve. After that, the game was over, and likely Dirisha would be in deep shit. The security program might have orders to inform Pen of unsuccessful attempts to peek at his files.

But, nothing risked, nothing gained—

ACKNOWLEDGED, the computer said.

Dirisha let her indrawn breath escape in a rush. Ha! So the inscrutable Pen wasn't omnipotent! She stabbed at the control of the projector, and sat in front of the terminal. She typed in the word "Index", and waited to see what secrets were hers for the taking.

FOURTEEN ———————

PEN'S PERSONAL FILES were extensive—there were hundreds of entries, detailing all kinds of fascinating things: biographies of students, names of local officials who had been bribed, a lengthy section on pubtending, even one entitled, "Love." It was interesting reading, but it did not reveal the reason behind it all. Aside from what Dirisha had been told, she could find no other, secret purpose.

Seated in front of the holoproj, working the terminal, Dirisha scanned a dozen files quickly. She read her own biograph. Some of it was written by Pen's agents, a multi-viewed accounting of her movements from the time she'd left Khadaji's employ on Greaves until she'd arrived on Renault. Other parts were evaluations by instructors at the Villa, including Pen's comments. She was, she noted, well-thought of.

Geneva's file carried comments similar to hers.

There were files on Bork, Sleel, Sister and even Khadaji. Dirisha didn't bother to read these.

There was no file listed for Pen.

Damn. All the effort she'd expended to break into Pen's personal files, and there was nothing here. It was possible he had hidden something within an innocuously-named document, much as Dirisha had hidden her doctored storage sphere, in plain sight. But there was no way she could find that kind of information unless she scanned all the material, not unless she was amazingly lucky. Dirisha did not trust luck.

Dirisha looked at the chronographic read built into the holoproj image. She'd been reading for almost two hours, and she'd only touched the surface. Well. She could come back, now that she knew she could get in. Given enough time, she could scan all the files. Yet, even as she thought it, she felt as if that would be a waste of time. She wouldn't find anything. Pen had no reason to suspect anybody could bypass his security checks to get to his files; if he held some dark secret, it did not seem to be stored within the computer's vast memory.

Could it be that Pen's—and Khadaji's—reasons for starting the school were as Pen had said? Nothing more? That seemed too simple—

The air pressure in the room altered. Dirisha still stared at the holoprojic image, but she was aware that the door to the study had opened. The locked door. She spun away from the image, her right spetsdöd leading—

"Find anything interesting?" Pen said, from his stance in the doorway.

She was caught!

Despite her sudden rush of guilt, she managed to smile. "Nothing worth mentioning," she was finally able to say.

Pen walked to the console. As Dirisha watched, he bent

and tapped in a code. "Program in ID stats on Dirisha Zuri," Pen said.

ACKNOWLEDGED. PROGRAMED.

"Good. Dirisha Zuri is to have open access to any files stored under my security mode."

ACKNOWLEDGED.

Pen cleared the computer again.

"Why did you do that?"

"There are two ways I could go," Pen said. "I could add in more security, eye scans, complex code words, things like that, and keep you from sneaking into my files again. That might lead you to think I had something to hide. Or, I could let you see anything you wanted. A matter of trust."

Dirisha shook her head. "I wonder why it is everybody is so damned trusting of me! I don't deserve it."

"Perhaps."

"I mean, look, I just broke into your private files. If I were you, I'd be more than a little upset."

Pen crinkled. "I'm not. It shows initiative."

"Shit. How did you know what I was doing?"

"A security rider on my index. It informs me whenever anybody breaks in."

"I should have known."

"You aren't the first to try it. Or, even to succeed."

That surprised Dirisha.

"A few have managed, including you."

Dirisha wanted to ask who had tried, but she didn't. If he'd wanted her to know, Pen would have mentioned names.

"I expect it," Pen continued. "We're not training robots here. People who don't want to know more than they're shown probably won't make very good galactic movers."

Dirisha stood and faced Pen. She was almost as tall as he was. "So that's it? You don't have any secrets, no un-recycled corpses stashed under your bed?"

"Perhaps," Pen said. "Everyone has secrets. But what I

told you about what we want to do here is straight. And
you're happy here, aren't you?"

Dirisha thought about that, but only for a moment. She
realized he was right: she *was* happy here. Pen might be
twisty and devious, but he was teaching her things. She
didn't know exactly what it was she had been drawn into,
but she was happier here than any place she had ever been.
As long as that was the case, what did the rest of it matter?

"Yeah," she said. "I'm happy here."

Pen's eyes crinkled at the edges, and he said, "Good. It
gets better."

Part Two

"By knowing things that exist, you can know that which does not exist."

Miyamoto Musashi

"There are three kinds of brains: the one understands things unassisted, the other understands things when shown by others, the third understands neither alone nor with the explanations of others."

Machiavelli

FIFTEEN ————————

TWO OF THE three new students were pretty good; the third, Massey, was superb. Dirisha watched him walk the pattern, nodding to herself. Only here for a week, already Massey could do eleven steps. Dirisha had seen him stripped in the weight room, and his musculature was outstanding, even compared to students who had been at the school for many months. The other two were good, but Massey had real potential. If his brain were as sharp as his body, he was going to make a hell of a matador.

Dirisha watched one of the other students stumble on the eighth step, and she smiled. After four years, she could walk the pattern blindfolded. Four years of daily practice had given her mastery of many things, including the Ninety-Seven Steps. Were she to return to her old paths, to the Musashi Flex, she would be ranked in the top dozen players within a matter of days. But she would never go back.

Pen appeared, and moved to stand by Dirisha, as she watched one of her top students lead the class.

Massey made it to the twelfth step. Dirisha could almost see his thoughts as he struggled to twist his body for the thirteenth move. There has to be a way, he'd be thinking. I've seen others do it, it is possible.

"What do you think of him?" Pen asked.

"He's very good. Excellent, in fact. Where did you find him?"

"Earth. He was supposedly a freelance industrial courier with anti-Confed leanings."

Dirisha had known Pen too long to let the single most important word in his sentence pass unchallenged. "Supposedly?"

With a twist that almost, but not quite unbalanced him, Massey made the thirteenth step. An interesting rendition; clumsy, but acceptable. The man grinned.

Pen nodded, eyes alive within the shadow of his hood. "His credentials were impeccable. A deep background check by one of my best agents came up clean. Massey was born of poor-but-honest terran stock, worked his way through school while helping to support his brother and two sisters, after their bio-parents were killed in a park panic. A political Independent, a Universal Eclectic, a hardworking man who tolerates the Confed because he has to."

Massey tried the next step, and fell. He returned to the beginning of the pattern. A fall anywhere always meant a return to the beginning, even if it were on the last step.

"Sounds perfect," Dirisha said.

Pen nodded, but said nothing.

Whatever Pen had been getting at still hung between them, the fugue of his words clear and unrevealing.

"What's wrong with him?"

Pen smiled, face hidden as always, but the expression

obvious to one who had known him as long as Dirisha had.
"He's a spy."

Massey quickly walked the first ten steps, pausing slightly
at the next. The other students on their own patterns were
no farther along than six or eight moves.

"A spy? For whom?"

"The Confed, of course. I'm not positive which agency,
but I suspect he's one of the *Soldatutmarkt*, sent by The
Wall."

Dirisha turned away from the students to look directly
at Pen. "Marcus Jefferson Wall?" She felt a touch of fear
along her spine, extending a cold finger into her bowels.

"The same."

"The Wall," Dirisha recited, "kingmaker and puppet-
master, in control of the Confederation President; likely the
most dangerous and powerful man alive."

"I'm glad to see you remember your lessons."

"You think Massey is a spy for *him,* and yet you let him
into the school?"

Pen glanced at Dirisha, then back at Massey, who was
essaying his fourteenth move once again. He said, "Yes."

"But—why?"

"Have you ever heard the expression, 'Better the devil
you know than the devil you don't know'?"

"No."

"We have graduated fifty-three matadors in the years
since the school opened, not counting those who have stayed
here to continue teaching. Those fifty-odd men, women and
mues now work for the richest, most powerful men, women
and mues in the galaxy, all of whom tend to be anti-Confed
in their leanings. So far, our matadors have thwarted a total
of thirty-nine assassination attempts successfully. Not a single client has been lost."

Massey managed the fourteenth move. Amazing. Dirisha
turned back toward Pen.

"It is the business of such men as Marcus Wall to know everything of importance. Assassinations, or the attempt of such against men who can buy and sell planets, come to his attention. He was bound to learn about us, sooner or later."

Dirisha nodded. "Granted. But why a spy?"

"It is not for those who hold power by the most twisted of means to do things in a straightforward manner. Besides, we piqued his interest in a more—ah—personal manner."

"How so?"

"We turned down his application for a matador."

"You turned down The Wall? Chang, Pen, that would have been a coup! To be able to put a bug in *his* ear—!"

"No. We do not want Wall under our protection. Ever."

Dirisha turned back to watch Massey. He was outstanding, but he was not going to get the next step on the pattern, not this day. He fell.

"We do not take applicants for matadors," Pen said. "The Wall suborned one of my agents to present Massey as a candidate, and made him attractive under the standards I am wont to use for final selections."

"How did you find out?"

Pen did not speak, only smiled.

Dirisha blinked, her green eyes going momentarily blank as she recalled a bit of doggerel about smaller fleas upon the backs of larger fleas, and so on, *ad infinitum.*

Was there anything Pen left to chance?

"So you allowed him to come here."

"As long as he is in place," Pen said, "it is unlikely The Wall will send another spy. At worst, he must figure, he will have a man with our training. At best, he may uncover some kind of threatening conspiracy. Who knows for sure what he thinks?"

Dirisha stared at Massey, who was doggedly returning to the beginning of the pattern again. She had the feeling

that Pen knew exactly what Marcus Wall thought. He might
well be the most powerful and dangerous man in the galaxy,
but she would not wish to be in his position with Pen as
his enemy.

Sleel was back from San Yubi; Dirisha stood next to him
at the range, watching him shoot. Sleel would toss an empty
stinger magazine into the air, then plink at it. He hit the
target eight times of ten, which made him slightly better
than an average marksman. That irritated him no end, for
Sleel did not like to be less than anybody at anything. That
he was gave him something to strive for; Sleel would never
be satisfied until he was the best at everything.

"How was the trip?" Dirisha asked.

Sleel shrugged noncommittally. "Fine."

Dirisha grinned and reached for a handful of empty magazines. The small stressplast units rattled as she grabbed
them, and tossed them offhandedly downrange. Almost as
an afterthought, Dirisha whipped her spetsdöds up and began firing. The magazines jumped as the darts pinged into
them. Five magazines, five hits.

Sleel glared at Dirisha. He said nothing, only clenched
his teeth together.

Poor Sleel. He was so predictable. Dirisha knew the way
to get to him was to one-up him. He couldn't stand it. He
had to get ahead, somehow.

"Yeah, well, I spent some time with Rajeem Carlos's
personal rep while I was on San Yubi. At the Three Fingers
Inn, the most exclusive resort in this system."

Dirisha made an impressed noise.

"Carlos is head of the Antag Union, you know. Number
one target for Confed sympathizers."

"Really?" Dirisha knew that, but when humoring Sleel,
it was best to pretend ignorance, so he could shine.

"Yeah. And it looks as if Carlos wants a matador. And

I will be handling the negotiations for him to come here *personally*, to see our operation."

That one stopped Dirisha cold. Pen was allowing a potential *client* to see the Villa? What was going on? First a spy, now a client? That didn't make any sense, not if he wanted any semblance of security.

Sleel smiled, feeling smug about himself again, no doubt.

Dirisha said, "Okay, thanks. If you want to sharpen your shooting, watch that jab. You need to move continuously on multiple or moving targets, more like a wave." Dirisha tossed another magazine over the range and shot it casually with her left spetsdöd.

Sleel watched her carefully. He nodded, as much thanks as he was apt to give.

Dirisha walked away from the range, toward her room. Every time she thought she had this place figured out, Pen did something new, to surprise her. Maybe that was what kept the Villa from growing dull around her. On the other hand, like Sleel, there were some things Dirisha wanted answers to, for her own peace of mind. This was, after all, her home, and she didn't want it changed *that* much.

Geneva walked from the fresher, naked. She stretched toward the ceiling, and bent to touch her toes. Dirisha smiled at her lover.

Geneva straightened. "Did you hear about the uplevel bigwheel coming to the school? R.M. Carlos?"

Dirisha frowned. "How did *you* hear that?"

"Bork told me. Mayli told him, she got it from Sleel."

"Damned comvine around here is faster than White Radio."

"You didn't know?"

"I knew," Dirisha said. "What I don't know is: why?"

Geneva dived at the bed, tucked into a roll, and bounced off her back up onto her feet again. She turned to face

Dirisha. "Massage my back and I'll tell you."

"I'll massage your butt!" Dirisha lunged at Geneva in mock anger.

"Eeek! I was only kidding! The scat is that Carlos wants a matador, but he wants to pick one himself. Pen told him, via Sleel, that we've got twenty-three almost ready to graduate. The Antag Union wants Carlos to get the best, since there have already been two assassination attempts, the second of which barely missed."

"Okay, come lie down, I'll rub your back."

Geneva did another dive at the bed, this time landing on her belly. "Really?"

"Yes, really, brat. What else have you heard?" Dirisha began to knead at the hard muscles of Geneva's upper back.

"Umm. Ohh. That feels so good. What else? Nothing much."

"Come on, I can tell by your voice that you aren't telling all."

Dirisha felt the woman under her hands tighten slightly. "Pen thinks all the matadors here should be willing to consider going with Carlos. He says the best ones are instructors, and it's important that we keep Carlos alive. Very important."

Dirisha dug deeper with her fingertips, but the slight tenseness persisted. "Pen hasn't said anything to you yet, has he?"

Geneva had her face pressed against the bedding, and her voice when it came was very small. "Sort of."

"Sort of?"

Geneva raised herself on one elbow, to stare at Dirisha. "He asked if I was ready to go into the field yet."

"And you said . . . ?"

"No,"

Not as long as I stay here, Dirisha thought. That was the unspoken reason, she knew. It wasn't her responsibility,

Dirisha also knew, but then again, it was. Geneva was no puppy, following her around; she was a bright, attractive woman, the best matador the training had produced. She could outshoot any one at the school with a spetsdöd, including Pen himself, Dirisha suspected. Geneva had the best record for assassination defenses in practice, could walk the pattern faster than anybody save Dirisha and Pen, and was liked by everybody who met her. And Geneva's love for her bound them both, even without Dirisha's reciprocation.

"Lie back down, I'll finish your back, brat."

Geneva smiled, and flopped back onto her face. It took so little to make someone in love happy.

As Dirisha massaged the other woman, she shook her head. It was a complex subject, love. She could see the effect it had on somebody like Geneva, the care and dedication it engendered. Almost everybody seemed to know about it, even Penn, with his computer file on "Love." And his cryptic mutterings about how powerful it was, even more so than fanaticism. She could see it, but she couldn't see it. Love: Dirisha thought. A thing she was never apt to know.

SIXTEEN ——————————

DIRISHA SAT IN the study, in front of the computer console. Carlos was coming to the school, an unprecedented event, a client being allowed at Matador Villa. She wanted to know about this man. She stroked the computer into life, and called up Pen's files.

Name:	Rajeem Marson Carlos
Height:	190 cm
Weight:	96 kilos, TS
Hair:	Red
Eyes:	Blue
Tap:	Human–Terra/Eng-Irish/Span
DOB:	1 Jan. 2323, TS
Father:	Flannery Manuel Carlos,
	International Pharmaceutical

Mother:	Jean Amis James Carlos, Principal Violin, Baton Negro Symphony, Baton Negro, Zillia, SA
Siblings:	Sister, Celise, DOB, 29 Nov. 2334, TS; Brother, Haldor, DOB 2320, TS; Half Sister, Jerace, (paternal sperm donation), DOB 2323, TS
Education:	New London Cast–3-6 Oxford Prep–6-16 Oxford–16-19, B.A. Pre-Theo Dublin Theological–19-23 D.D., Catholic Humanistic Unitarianism, Ordained 23 June 2349, Full Prebendary.
Work:	Prebendary - a) Souva, Fiji, Republic of Oceanica

                                          b) Needles, CA
                              United World State America
                                          c) Barley, Titan
                                          d) Sparks,
                              Small Continent, Koji, Heiwa
                              System
                              Resigned Priesthood, 36
                              Joined Jeffersonian Conclave, 38
                              Joined Antag Union, 42
                              Elected President Antag Union, 44

Dirisha stared at the stats. Not much there, only the bare bones of what Carlos might be. One could interpret the facts, of course, but the accuracy of such would be suspect. Carlos had been a cleric, he'd quit, and joined a couple of organizations which offered token—and carefully legal— resistance to the Confederation dinosaur. Likely he was another one of the countless do-gooders who wanted things to be better but had few ideas or means to accomplish it.

A wisher, rather than a doer. Dirisha had met such men in her travels, well-meaning souls busy paving the roads to their particular hells. Well. It didn't really matter—she wasn't leaving the school to be his keeper.

There was an assembly, to meet the great man. Dirisha stood near the back of the auditorium, watching Massey, the spy. If ever a man should be safe from attack, it ought to be here, but Massey was a question mark. He might be willing to take out Carlos, if it could be blamed on the school.

The leader of the Antag Union arrived, smiling and talking with Pen as he walked. He was a big man, with flaming red hair set in a conservative cut, wearing an uninteresting gray business tunic and trousers, his feet shod in custom-spun dotic boots to match his clothes. He and Pen were surrounded by a retinue, all Carlos's people, since Dirisha recognized none of them. Four of the party looked to be accountants or advisors; the final pair were obviously body-guards. Dirisha focused her attention on the last two men, both of whom were large, easy-moving, and constantly watching the sixty or so students in the auditorium, eyes shifting alertly. Weapons, if they carried them, were well-hidden. They weren't bad, but not in the same class as a matador. The taller of the bodyguards was an attractive man who looked oddly pale, his blue eyes and skin tone not matching his black hair. Well. Dirisha could hardly fault his genetics, with her own green eyes and black skin.

As the group passed Dirisha, she glanced away, to check Massey's position, and so almost missed the second clue. She looked back at Carlos, who leaned over to say something to Pen, and his gaze met hers for a second. He smiled, showing nice crinkle lines at the edges of his green eyes. He and Pen could go into business and make a fortune, they could sell the secret to those smile lines—

Dirisha's own smile stopped. The group reached the sunken stage, and Pen began to speak. The focused microcaster amplified his voice so that it filled the auditorium. Dirisha listened with half her attention: she was busy watching the black-haired, blue-eyed bodyguard.

"—are honored by the visit of Rajeem Carlos of the Antag Union," Pen said. "Prebendary Carlos has traveled a long way—"

Dirisha spared Massey a glance, saw he was watching Carlos intently, and grinned. Carlos was in no danger. Pen knew who Massey was, after all, even if she was wrong. But she didn't think she was. Oh, it was possible, of course, such slim clues, but they were just the kind of thing Pen loved to use. Skin stain was cheap, and droptacs could do miracles, if they were serious; but if she were right, Pen was practically flaunting it, and she couldn't let him get away with it, they'd never hear the end of it.

"—will be observing our training for the next few days. Feel free both to comment to him candidly, and ask him questions."

There was her opening. Dirisha strode down the aisle until she was only a few meters away from the speaker's platform. Pen spotted her. "Dirisha?"

She looked at the red-haired man. "Do you wear droptacs, Prebendary Carlos?"

The man looked startled. "Why, no. Why do you ask?"

Dirisha looked at Pen, and grinned. Under his cowl, he grinned back. She shifted her gaze away and to the black-haired bodyguard. The man regarded her calmly, with a hint of humor in his blue eyes. "Then I'd like to welcome you to Matador Villa, on behalf of the students."

Several students laughed behind her, as they understood what she was doing.

Pen said, "How many of you knew, before Dirisha spoke?"

Dirisha turned. No hands were raised.

"How many of you still don't know?"

Two dozen hands were raised.

Pen nodded at Dirisha. "Clues?"

"The obvious ones—eyes and skin tone."

Pen walked three steps to his left, and stood next to the bodyguard. "Students and instructors, *this* is Prebendary Rajeem Carlos." He gestured at the bodyguard. "And the man smiling at you over there is an imposter. How many of you read the dossier on Pr. Carlos before he arrived?"

All but a few hands were raised.

"Good, I expected no less. But I am disappointed that more of you failed to see the ruse. Congratulations, Dirisha."

Dirisha acknowledged Pen's compliment, then looked at the real Carlos. The man smiled broadly, and Dirisha felt a stirring of something within her. He was attractive, not really handsome, but she could feel his *ki* flowing forth powerfully. Not at all what she had thought he would be from his file. In his close-fitting clothing, she could see his frame was well-muscled, hardly what she'd expected.

The galaxy was just full of surprises.

The winters on this part of Renault were mild; enough so that Dirisha only wore a light jacket over her orthoskins as she walked through the scrubby trees a klick away from the school. She'd explored this area dozens of times in the last few years, but each time seemed to bring her a taste of the new. Today, there was a sense of something impending, a feeling of tension, as if the air were full of positive ions, awaiting the release of a cleaning storm.

Past the scrub was an irregular ring of waxy-leaved evergreen bushes, two meters tall, a brooding green against the stark winterscape. Dirisha would sometimes sit and meditate

within the circle of thick vegetation, for the bushes absorbed
wind and sound well enough to give the enclosed space a
relaxing stillness.

Today, when she approached the circle, Dirisha felt the
presence of another within, the *ki* of someone she had come
to know. So she was not surprised when she saw Pen sitting
seiza near the center of the grove of evergreens. That he
was waiting for her, she doubted not at all.

Dirisha knelt across from Pen a meter and a half away
and settled onto her heels, a mirror of his pose. She waited.

After a moment, Pen spoke.

"You saw Carlos before you left the school." Not a question.

"Yes. He was watching Twisp and Kaynon at the range.
Red had them working against simulacrums in class-two
military armor. Carlos pretended to be most impressed with
their ability to find the small cracks in the armor's joints
with their spetsdöd slugs."

"Pretended to be," Pen said. Again, it was not a question,
but a flat statement.

Dirisha took a deep breath. "Yes. He's been here for
three days, poking around the classes, nodding sagely at
what he sees, making appropriate noises to show he's impressed. It's all a sham, isn't it?"

Pen deflected the question with one of his own. "What
do you think of him?"

"He's not what I expected."

A stray breeze found its way past the surrounding bushes
and ruffled Pen's robe slightly. His gaze seemed locked on
Dirisha, his blue eyes unblinking against the cool wind. He
said, "Carlos is a very important man. More so than you
imagine. The Confed is losing its war to stay in control,
you know that, but the end is much nearer than almost
anyone realizes. It will fall soon, and Rajeem Carlos will
be a major force among the ruins—if he survives the col-

lapse. There are hundreds, thousands of people who might rise from the ashes as brilliant lights, many who would lead mankind along a different path, one of peace and non-violence, but Carlos is one of the brightest and best. We must not lose him."

"I understand what you're saying," Dirisha said. "But your fugue escapes me."

"I don't think it does, Dirisha."

Dirisha met Pen's gaze with her own, but focused past him, thinking. She was pretty sure she understood at least part of what Pen meant. She said, "Carlos has already made his choice. The rest of his visit is just window dressing."

Pen nodded, once.

Dirisha took a deep breath, and tried to quell the fluttering in her belly. The sensation would not go away. There could only be one reason for Pen's presence here, and his oblique word dance. She shook her head. "I'm not interested."

Pen said nothing, only kept staring at her.

"I'm not the best, Pen. If you want that, send Geneva with him." That thought wasn't comfortable, either. She had grown more than fond of Geneva, even if she didn't love her.

"Geneva did not see through the disguise."

"Is that what impressed him? It was luck, Pen—"

"No, it wasn't. It was part of a . . . design."

Dirisha rose from the kneeling pose to her feet, turning away from Pen to stare at the encircling greenery. This place had become her home, she didn't want to leave, didn't want any changes. There was a kind of security here, more than she'd ever felt before. She had friends here. To leave would be to lose that; she couldn't. She wouldn't. She turned back to face Pen.

He was gone.

Dirisha felt a stab of panic. She darted to the perimeter of the glade, searching for him, but he was not to be seen.

For a moment, Dirisha was afraid she had hallucinated him, but when she touched the ground where Pen had knelt, the earth was warm.

She stood alone in the clearing for a long time after Pen vanished, thinking. Her mind was filled with turmoil. What was his comment about her luck being part of a design all about? True, Dirisha felt drawn to Carlos somehow, as if he were comfortable and familiar in a way she couldn't put a finger on, but even Pen's manipulations couldn't extend that far. She'd never met the man before, never seen him or known much of anything about him until she read his file. Even Pen couldn't see the future, or tell how somebody would react to another person. Or could he? She remembered his talk to her about Geneva, the day they'd gone walking together. He had been pretty sure Geneva would fall in love with her, hadn't he? Damn, what was Pen up to? What devious game did he have her playing? She could not shake the feeling that she was a puppet, and that her strings had just been pulled, carefully and expertly; that no matter what she did, Pen would expect it.

Damn!

SEVENTEEN ———————

NINE ARMED SIMULACRA charged Dirisha, crowding each other in the confines of the shooting range. Nine was the limit of the viral intelligence that created the ersatz-reality of the combat range, and nobody had ever beaten that many opponents at once.

Dirisha dodged, rolled, fired, leaped, fired again and again, filling the air with the sounds of her spetsdöds. She was good . . . but she wasn't that good. On her seventh hit, she side-stepped a throwing steel, only to feel the tingle of a particle spitter. Seven out of nine, not bad, but dead was dead. She shut down the range, disgusted. No, it wasn't so much disgust as it was anger. She felt a rage, and she reached for the simulacrum control, intending to dial up another half-dozen attackers, unarmed ones this time. She wanted to kick something. Or somebody.

She became aware of another presence as she touched the control. Geneva. Dirisha turned, away from the generator, to look at her friend and lover.

"I take it you've heard?" Dirisha said.

Geneva nodded. Her face looked grave.

"Don't look so gloomy, brat. I'm not going anywhere."

Geneva waved a hand at the firing range. "Why are you so upset?"

Dirisha considered that. She had been considering it ever since she had spoken to Pen in the clearing earlier. She wasn't sure she knew. But she decided to try to express it. "Pen's twisty mind," she said. "I get the feeling he expected me to see through the bodyguard switch; that he expected Carlos to decide he wanted me for a guard; that there are things going on here I haven't begun to see. I feel like a chess pawn, a single *Go* stone, without an inkling of the over-all strategy of the larger game."

Geneva moved closer, so that she could reach out and touch Dirisha. She did so, stroking the older woman's face with the trembling fingers of one hand. The beginnings of tears pooled in Geneva's eyes, and she said, "I think you should consider going with Carlos."

Dirisha was shocked. Geneva was the last person she'd expect to say that! "You want me to leave?"

The twin pools of tears brimmed and overflowed. "No. Oh, no. More than anything in the universe, I want you to stay."

"But . . . ?"

"But Pen does understand things you and I don't. All this—" she waved to encompass Matador Villa "—all this is important in some larger plan, that I do know. If Pen thinks Rajeem Carlos is so valuable a person that he wants the best of us to protect him, there must be a good reason."

Dirisha raised her hand and touched Geneva's arm. "Hon, *I'm* not the best, you are—"

"No," Geneva interrupted. "I can shoot a little straighter or faster, maybe, but there's something in you I don't have, Dirisha, a kind of . . . depth—"

"Shit there is—"

"It's true. Pen can see it."

Dirisha turned away, to stare at the firing range. After a moment, she turned back to face Geneva, who was crying soundlessly, the tears streaming and falling from her face. "Did he talk to you? Pen?"

Geneva nodded.

"Damn him! And are you supposed to convince me to zip off with Carlos."

"I said I'd talk to you."

Dirisha wanted to scream. That Pen would use Geneva this way was reprehensible! He knew the girl was in love with her, that she would do anything in Dirisha's best interest. Dammit, he had gone too far!

Dirisha hugged Geneva to her. "Easy, hon. I'm going to have a little talk with Pen, you just don't worry about anything, you hear? Just don't worry."

Pen sat behind his desk as Dirisha stormed into the office. The man in gray was playing with a curved knife, shaped much like a plantain, a thing of mirror steel, polished brass and close-grained wood. It seemed nothing so much as a fang to Dirisha, a steel tooth from some mechanical monster.

"Ah," Pen said. "I've been expecting you. Sit down."

"I'll stand," Dirisha said, barely holding her anger in check.

Pen continued to twirl the knife; light reflected from the blade, glinting against the cool walls. After a moment, Pen held the knife up, staring at it. "This was part of Emile Khadaji's training," Pen said. "A lesson in basics, about how even simple things can be very important." He looked away from the blade, at Dirisha, and set the knife upon his desk. "You remember the first time you came into this office."

"I remember. Listen, I don't think much of what you did to Geneva—"

"I told you then we had something here you hadn't found in the Flex," Pen continued, ignoring Dirisha's interruption. "It's been almost five years. Was I right?"

Dirisha's anger threatened to erupt, but she nodded tightly. "You know you were."

"You've been happy here. Satisfied?"

"Yes, dammit—"

"Have you ever stopped to wonder how most of the people in the galaxy feel about their lives? If they are satisfied? If the ever-present fear of the Confederation monster haunts even their dreams? No, I suppose you haven't. Emile Khadaji did, and he was willing to spend his life to do something about it. He's been an inspiration for resistance fighters everywhere, the man who took on an army."

"I know that, Pen—"

"We sit here in our comfort, wanting for nothing, while evil is done. To not do something about it is immoral, Dirisha. You have had five years of rest, of peace, of training. Don't you think it's time you paid your dues? Put that training and skill to use?"

Dirisha found her anger dissipating. What Pen said had occurred to her before. She had been given a free ride, paid to become better, faster, happier. Had she really thought she deserved it, for nothing in return? No. It didn't work that way. You had to earn what you got, always.

"You can stay here as long as you wish," Pen continued. "But I wonder if you can stay, knowing that by being elsewhere you could do something important, something worthwhile? Something beyond yourself, for the first time. Something to help your fellow human beings to find a better path than the one they are now forced to tread."

Dirisha moved to the only other chair in the room, and sat. Helping the sheep meant nothing; playing by her own rules did, and honor was one of those rules. You pay for what you get and you don't owe anybody. She didn't want to leave this place, not ever, it was the home she'd never had as a child, but she owed for it. Pen had called her on it, and Dirisha knew she couldn't ignore that particular call. *You owe us, Dirisha, and the time has come to pay.*

Okay. Okay.

"I think what you did with Geneva sucks vac, Pen. I think you've gotten so used to manipulating people you think you're some kind of god, it doesn't matter what you're doing it for, in the long run. I don't think you care about anybody or anything, save this serpentine game you're playing."

For a moment, she saw pain touch his eyes, and she fancied she could see through the opaque shroud he always wore in public, to a face twisted in regret. Then the moment was gone, and the unperturbable, inscrutable mask returned.

"But you'll take the job with Carlos?"

"Yeah, I'll take the goddamned job."

There was a graduation ceremony, of a sort. Dirisha had attended dozens, without ever really thinking she'd be the woman onstage someday. Early on, maybe, she'd wanted that, but later, once the school became home, that had changed. It wasn't that elaborate a set-up, no big deal.

Still, there was something about it that Dirisha found . . . stirring. Matadors usually graduated one at a time, people learned at different speeds, and Pen was always one for precision. You left when you and he thought you were ready.

Standing on the stage in front of the assembled students, Dirisha knew that she and Pen both knew she had been ready for a long time. She just hadn't reached the leaping off point on her own.

Pen flowed onto the stage, as smooth as usual, dressed as always. Dirisha wore a new set of gray orthoskins, newly spun dotic boots, and both spetsdöds. It was Khadaji's uniform, the same kind as he had worn on Greaves, and while there was no rule against it, no graduating matador or matadora ever wore anything else. The imagery was clear: when you hired a matador, you were hiring somebody cast in the same mold as Emile Antoon Khadaji, the Man Who Never Missed. Quite a selling point, from what Dirisha knew. The only difference was the shoulder patch, a hand-sized, bright red holographic splotch, shaped like a small cape. Floating over the cape was an androgynous human figure, dressed in a kind of tight-fitting coverall. A suit of lights, Pen called it, worn only by the original matadors of Old Earth.

Pen moved to stand next to Dirisha. The already-quiet room grew tangibly more so, as if no one dared even breathe.

Pen faced the audience. "You all know Dirisha," he said, "and you all know she is more than ready to graduate as a fully-operational matadora. Her time has come to leave."

Dirisha scanned the assembly. There was Geneva. Tears ran freely down the blonde's face, but she was smiling.

"Dirisha has an important client. He is getting the best Matador Villa has to offer. She will be missed."

Pen turned toward Dirisha. From his robe, he produced a biomed popper, the size of a fingertip, and handed it to her. That was the FTS virus all graduates received.

Dirisha nodded her thanks.

Pen pulled another small item from the cloth depths of his shroud. A galactic stad cube. She was well-off when

she'd come to the Villa, she was more so now. Whatever
she had was joined in her account now by her first year's
salary—each year was paid by the client in advance, refundable if the client should terminate a matador's ser-
vices—or if the client was terminated.

Pen extended his hand, bearing the third and final item
each graduate received. Two items, actually. A pair of spetsdöd magazines, loaded with live ammunition. No longer
the blunt-tipped darts for Dirisha; she was now immune to
practice attack by students. Were she to return fire now, the
shock-tox flechettes she would load wouldn't kill, but they
would do much more than sting.

One at a time, she unloaded and reloaded her weapons.
She half expected Pen to try a final salvo at her before she
switched over—he had done it to one about-to-graduate
student and kept him in-house another three months when
the man couldn't return fire fast enough. But Pen made no
threatening moves. In a few seconds, the practice rounds
were unloaded and replaced.

She jiggled the magazines in her hand, as if weighing
them, or shaking dice. The matador patch on her shoulder
seemed to flash in the quiet room, the suit of lights against
the red background gleaming like thousands of pinpoint
precious stones. Dirisha felt a flutter within her; it was as
if she suddenly felt a kinship with those ancient matadors.
The ammunition, the patch, the virus, they were all tangible
proof that she was no longer simply a student.

Dirisha squeezed the small bits of plastic in her hand
tightly. Then, she threw the old magazines into the crowd,
slinging them high into the air. The school was only a few
years old, but it had its traditions. Whoever caught the
magazines were supposed to be the next two to graduate.
A field of hands rose as the magazines flew, and there was
a break in the silence as the students yelled and laughed.

Dirisha smiled, both elated and sad. She glanced at Pen, then back at the assembly. One of the magazines was held by Barthal Jinks, a student only three months into the training. So much for tradition. When she looked to see who had the second, it took a moment. And it shook her, when she finally saw. Her smile died, and her stomach seemed to clutch itself.

Geneva, unsmiling, held the second magazine.

During the going away party, Sleel got drunk on vör-emhölts and tried to throw Bork across the room, which resulted in Sleel pulling a groin muscle. Mayli danced an erotic dance, which sent half the party in search of places to consummate the lust which resulted. Red, toked on kick-dust, staged an exhibition of point shooting, picking matches from a pile on a table top with his spetsdöd, never moving a match other than the one he shot at, never scratching the clear plastic finish of the table.

It was a fine party, nearly everybody had a wonderful time.

Throughout the buzz of happy conversation and revelry, Dirisha moved, smiling and nodding at well-wishers, always aware of Geneva watching her every move. Dirisha wanted the party to last forever, for every moment thus occupied delayed the moment she dreaded: being alone with Geneva.

Bork nearly crushed her with his farewell embrace. "Uh, we'll miss you, Dirisha. It won't be the same without you."

Mayli kissed her, teacher to student, sister to sister, friend to friend. "Learn joy," she said.

Even Sleel seemed at a loss for something clever, and only managed a lame wisecrack: "You got a few minutes, Dirisha, last chance to know ecstasy before you take off." She was almost tempted, to see how he would perform with that particular set of muscles injured the way they were, but she settled for a hug and an almost-brotherly kiss.

Pen was nowhere to be seen, and as the party wound down, students drifting away, Dirisha found herself standing in front of Geneva. The blonde was dry-eyed and wore a fixed smile. Dirisha extended one hand, and Geneva took it, clutching it as a falling woman might grab at a dangling rope.

"You want to go back to the room?"

Geneva shook her head. "I—I don't think I could do that."

Dirisha tried a smile, saw the effort Geneva was expending to hold herself together, and let the expression fade. "Hon, I'm sorry. I wish there was some way I could make this easier for you. You've been closer to me than anybody in my life, a friend far beyond that of a lover. I'll miss you more than anybody else here."

Geneva drew in a deep breath, nearly a sob. "I'm leaving, too."

Dirisha blinked. Leaving?

"Pen found a client for me. Ambassador Teiki, of Hadiya. I'll be spending a lot of time on Earth, at the Confederation Embassy Compound."

"That's good," Dirisha said. In truth, she felt saddened. Knowing Geneva was here made it easier to leave. The idea of being gone forever hadn't sunk in yet. Most of them would probably go someday, she had known that, but it had never seemed real before.

The two women held hands, standing alone in the room. They didn't speak for a long time. Finally, Geneva said, "I will always love you, Dirisha. Across a thousand light years and forever, I will never stop loving you."

Dirisha gathered Geneva into her arms and hugged her tightly, inhaling the scent of the blonde where she pressed her face against the fine, golden hair. *I'll miss you, too, brat, in ways I've never missed anybody or anything.* "You will always be in my heart, Geneva. Always."

As Dirisha walked toward the rail car, she looked around at the school with an intensity she had never known before. How odd to be leaving, maybe forever. It still didn't feel real.

Several students were working out in the chilly morning air, walking the patterns imprinted upon the rockfoam. They appeared to take no notice of Dirisha as she left. No one had come to see her off, which was just as well. Her sadness didn't need more fuel. Leaving was strange enough without tearful farewells in the cold light of day.

Dirisha had all her belongings in the same bag she'd carried when she'd arrived nearly five years earlier; that hadn't changed. A lot of other things were different, though. She wasn't the same person who'd come here.

The rail car beckoned, a few meters ahead. Dirisha sighed as she approached the door to the small vehicle. Better to do this fast, get in and go, before she got caught up in the emotions which bubbled around in the back of her head. She tossed her bag through the open door, and bent to enter the car.

"Dirisha," came the voice from behind her.

She turned.

Pen stood there, wrapped in his grayness, eyes alive in the shadow of his hood. Dirisha was surprised, and surprised at herself for being so—anything Pen did should not be unexpected by this time.

"Good-bye, Dirisha, and good luck."

Dirisha shook her head. "Thanks, Pen. I think."

Then he did something else Dirisha never expected. He walked to her and hugged her. "Take care," he said. "You are a more valuable person than you know."

As the rail car pulled away from Matador Villa, Dirisha

stared through the back window at the solitary figure of Pen, the wind ruffling his robes as he stood next to the track, watching her leave. The figure seemed to blur a lot sooner than it should, as though she were watching it through eyes that had somehow suddenly malfunctioned. There must be something wrong with her droptacs, she thought, as she wiped her face. She couldn't be crying.

EIGHTEEN ———————

As THE BOXCAR flew toward the terminal in high orbit, Dirisha began to itch. All over. The sensation wasn't new, she had felt it before during micro-term augmentation, but it was lessened none for that. The itching was caused by the presence of multiplying colonies of genetically-altered neurological bacteria. When fully circulating, such symbiotic flora would increase the neuroconductive speed of its host by as much as a factor of two. Normally, such reflex-aug biologicals were restricted to special units of Confed Military; as in most restricted things, however, a black market had developed. It cost, but it could be had. Pen had a bandit bio-unit on retainer, and upon graduation from the school, each matador was given an injection of the bacteria-aug. There was a long chemical-biological name for the substance, but it had been dubbed FTS by some wit some-

where along the line—FTS standing for "faster than shit."
The colonies were self-limited and short-lived at best, and
had to be renewed once or twice a year.

So Dirisha itched, but managed to stand it, as the boxcar
achieved orbit and jockeyed toward the terminal where she
was to catch a Bender ship for Wu, in the Haradali System.
Wu was another mainly agro world, only partially developed, and the planet where Carlos and the headquarters of
the Antag Union were. Dirisha had done a viral-inject learning cap about Wu, so she knew what there was available
to know about it.

Rajeem Carlos was already there by now, waiting for his
new matador to arrive.

"Arriving Renault Space Terminal," came a mechanical
voice over Dirisha's seat. "Docking in five minutes."

Dirisha touched a flat bar under the viewer inset into the
seat in front of her. A holoproj test pattern appeared. She
stroked the control through a series of channels, until a view
of Renault appeared, a globe the size of a basketball floating
over her lap. The planet was shrouded in lacy clouds, a blue
sphere with a slash of rusty black on one side, where a
chain of extinct volcanic mountains rose from a vast plain
of crumbling lava. There, to the south, would be Simplex-
by-the-Sea, so tiny at this distance as to be invisible, pop-
ulated by microbes.

Dirisha sighed, and shut off the projection. It had been
even harder to go than she'd expected. On the other hand,
there was a certain anticipation, a fluttery thrill in her belly,
when she thought about Carlos. And the work, of course,
being able to put her skills to use in actuality, instead of
mere school testing.

"Docking in two minutes," came the voice again.

Dirisha put away her memories and anticipation, and
gathered up her bag and a small reader. In a few hours, she

would be in deep space, being bent to a world billions of kilometers away.

"We are now docking at the Renault Space Terminal. Please remain seated until linkage and pressure lock are complete. Have a nice trip, and thank you for slinging on Renault Extraplanetary Spaceways."

The Bender ship was much like an ocean liner in its interior construction; externally, however, it was a disaerodynamic squarish block, since it would never touch a planet's atmosphere. In the between space traversed by a Bender, not even wisps of interstellar hydrogen existed to produce drag, and so any vessel shape was as good as the next.

Dirisha spent most of her time in the ship's gym or shooting range, occasionally stripping, save for her spetsdöds, to swim laps in the exercise pool. She turned down nine offers to copulate during the first three days of the voyage, along with six invitations to dine and one proposal of short-term marriage. As was the case in many of her past trips, she noted the large numbers of idle rich, Confederation officials and rootless travellers onboard

Twice, Dirisha saw Flex players trying to surreptitiously watch her. Both times, the players declined to issue challenges. She smiled at that; her skills and new speed made her too dangerous, and they were good enough to see that, fortunately for them. She was tempted to call one of the players out, but recognized the desire as a childish one. It would be a slaughter, and there was no joy to be taken in that. Besides, she was out of it now, such minor stakes held no interest for her. That thought was a surprise when she had it, and it made her feel good. She had bigger fields to harvest, and small contentions were not a part of her world any more.

The trip took three weeks, T. S., and by the time the

ship returned to normal space, Dirisha was more than ready
to begin her new job. She was eager.

"You'd be Zuri," the man said, disdain in his voice.

Dirisha nodded. "Yes." She looked at the man, and recalled where she'd seen him before: he was one of Carlos's
bodyguards, with him at Matador Villa. A big man, he was,
hard and dangerous, more so because he now felt threatened.

They stood in the lee of a bank of lockers in the ground
building of the boxcar terminal. Gusts of wind moaned
against the lockers from an open door across the large room,
warm wind bearing the foreign smells of a new planet.

Dirisha decided to put this on a professional basis immediately. The contract with a matador stipulated that he
or she was to be in complete charge of a client, and any
other security personnel were to be under the command of
the matador. "Who is watching Pr. Carlos?"

The big man seemed to mull that one over for a moment
before he answered. "Starboard is with him. Grandle Diggs."

That would likely be the impersonator she'd seen at the
school. Nicknamed 'Starboard'?

"Then you'd be called 'Port', right?"

He nodded. "Tork Ramson."

Dirisha said, "Let me guess: you always cover the left,
and Starboard always covers the right."

Port looked surprised. "Yeah."

Dirisha shook her head. She'd bet these two clowns were
standard security issue, probably running simple set patterns
that never varied. It was a wonder Carlos was still alive.
She said as much to Port.

"Hey, listen sister, we've been keeping him alive for three
years—!"

"A miracle, in any faith. Now you listen up, Port. You've
got your job as long as you do what I tell you. The first
time you fuck up or drag your heels or even look surly,

you're gone, copy? There are people who want this man dead, and it isn't going to happen while I'm running the show."

Port looked as if he were ready to take a swing. Dirisha almost wanted him to, but decided it would be better to impress him without undue violence. Before he could move, she stepped around him, her faster reflexes kicking in so that he seemed to be moving in slow motion. She jabbed Port lightly just under the seventh vertebrae of his thick spine with the barrel of her spetsdöd, printing a small circle into his flesh. He froze.

"I'm loading heavy shock-tox darts," she said, "and if I let one go, you'll spend a very unpleasant two hours wishing you could die, Port. I was hired because I'm one of the best there is at this business, that's no scat, just plain fact. Do we understand each other?"

She heard Port swallow dryly. He nodded. "Yes, Fem Zuri."

Dirisha moved her hand away from Port's back. "Good. Now, let's go see our employer."

Dirisha was appalled at how easy it was to get to Carlos. Port led her past a single guard holding a .177 Parker at port-arms, through an unarmored gate that a strong man or mue could have kicked open. The guard glanced at the carrier with Port and Dirisha inside, and waved them through without a word, much less a security scan. Dirisha felt her stomach knot. There were so many ways to gain entrance here she didn't bother to start thinking of them. That system would be changed before the day was out.

There were several small buildings surrounding the headquarters of the Antag Union, itself a blocky structure with more glass than stone in its walls, four stories tall. One terrorist with a vacuum bomb could bring the place down like a house of twigs. Chang, didn't these people know *any*thing?

At the lobby entrance, one guard again, an old woman wearing an antique explosive pellet pistol. Couldn't they at least give her a shotgun or hand wand? The woman nodded at Port, and didn't ask who Dirisha was. Gods.

Up the tube to the second floor. Down a hallway to a plain door. Well, that was one way to do it, hide the client. Except that the big man sitting at the door looking bored was a dead revelation. Starboard. He smiled. Then he must have seen the scowl on Port's face, for Starboard's grin faded in a hurry.

"He in?" Port asked.

"Yeah. 'Less he went to the pissor."

"You remember Fem Zuri," Port said. "He wanted to see her as soon as I brought her back."

"Sure. Go on in."

Dirisha's earlier decision about keeping Port and Starboard changed. They resented her, and they were incompetent. A possibly lethal combination for her client.

Prebendary Rajeem Carlos stood next to the lighted stall of a *betydelse* space, blinking. He must have just finished, for he wore that confused, vulnerable look operators often had during post-transmit/receive fugue.

A floor-to-ceiling window behind Carlos allowed the afternoon sun to paint the room in a warm yellow; aside from the *betydelse* space, the room held a standing desk, a computer terminal, a short couch and a file cabinet.

Carlos wore a gray business coverall and his feet were bare, against the thick brown carpet.

"I brought her," Port said, his voice barely civil.

Carlos blinked again, a night creature unused to daylight, and squinted at Dirisha. A smile lit his face. "Ah, Fem Zuri! I've been looking forward to your arrival."

Dirisha acknowledged Carlos with a choppy, military bow. "Could we speak privately, Prebendary?"

"Rajeem, please. Certainly. Would you mind waiting outside, Tork?"

Port turned wordlessly and stalked out.

Dirisha shook her head at the broad smile Carlos wore. He looked genuinely happy. She hated to kill that smile, but she had her job to do. "Prebendary—Rajeem—if I were an assassin, even one with as little skill as a prepube at play, you would certainly be dead by now. Your bodyguards and your security are a not-funny joke. I could have been holding a gun on Port, to force him to bring me here—nobody challenged us! A determined killer could have shot his way in almost as easily, past that spit-shined trooper at the gate and your great-grandmother downstairs, and Starboard on the door would've had to wait for signals from his hindbrain before he moved, by which time you'd be history and the assassin would be halfway across the galaxy. And that window you're standing in front of—move away from there! There could be a shooter with a wire or radio-opped cruiser two klicks away, waiting for a chance to take out this room or the whole building, for that!"

If she thought to scare him or make him angry, Dirisha was wrong. His smile, if anything, grew. "Yes, m'lady," he said, moving obediently away from the window. "How nice to see you again."

For a moment, Dirisha felt disarmed in her argument. How could she be angry with him? He was a religious man, not a matador; more, that smile was infectious. She fought her own grin, barely holding it back.

"Surely things are not as bad as all that?" he said.

There was an underlying, unspoken laughter that seemed to mock her. Not maliciously, but it was as if Carlos held some terribly funny secret. As if she were being tested again.

Suspicion dawned on Dirisha.

She walked to the window and tapped it lightly with the

barrel of her left spetsdöd. The clink! told her what she thought was true. The window wasn't glass or plastic, it was stressed densecris, and a good two centimeters thick. That it was so clear and did not distort the light testified to the expense of the armor. Forget the cruise attack, then. No small firepower was coming through that window.

It had to be more than that, though. Somebody with enough sense to install densecris and to hire a matador wouldn't leave much else to chance. Dirisha turned back toward Carlos, feeling the beginnings of chagrin.

"The gate," she said.

"Electrified and rigged with explosive bolts," Carlos said. "Capable of stopping any ground vehicle short of a class two megatruck. The guard's shack contains enough scanning gear to pick up bone nails."

"The old woman?"

"The pistol isn't what it seems. A wide-beam hand wand. And she's backed by three young women masquerading as secretaries. And the tube's controls are mislabeled—this is the third floor, not the second."

"Port and Starboard are not, I take it, as slow-witted or easy to anger as they appear."

"They *are* fair actors; I'm sure you'll like their real personalities."

"But there's more," Dirisha said.

Carlos nodded. "Pen said you were the best. I'm a fair hand at kung-fu, first degree sifu in rank."

Dirisha chewed on what Carlos had just told her. "All of this is very sophisticated. Who set it up?"

Carlos's smile returned.

"That's what I thought," Dirisha said. "Why did he send me, if he gave you all this?"

"If you had known about my security set-up, could you have figured a way to get to me anyway?"

"Eventually," Dirisha said without hesitation. "Any system can be bypassed."

"That's why Pen wanted you to help me. He told me you'd start to figure it out before I told you."

Dirisha shook her head again. Damn, Pen seemed to know everything about everything. Light years away, and he was still standing just behind her, laughing silently under his gray robes.

Carlos extended a hand. Automatically, Dirisha took it. She felt a rush as his fingers touched her, as a flock of butterflies took flight in her stomach. What was it about him that affected her this way? There was no denying the attraction, just as Dirisha was certain Pen knew of it. What was Pen up to? Just why had he set her up with Rajeem Carlos? Well. It didn't matter. She wasn't a broadcast toy, her will was her own, that much was certain. She didn't have to play Pen's game, she didn't want to. The problem, as always with Pen, lay in figuring out what his game *was*.

"Come on," Carlos said. "I'll show you around."

Dirisha nodded.

NINETEEN ————————————

SETTING UP HER first-stage security arrangements for Carlos was easier than she'd first anticipated. Pen's system was first class, and both Port and Starboard were adept at their jobs. While the Confed would have loved to see Rajeem Carlos messily dead, it had apparently made no overt moves in that direction. Carlos explained that to her, as they ate breakfast in his home.

"The Confed is so busy swatting larger flies it can't afford the time and energy to swat one so apparently harmless as I. Too many hindbrains, I suspect." He bit into a soft roll, chewed and swallowed. "And the Antag Union is not without allies in high places. So, for now, no direct action. If they should ever clean up enough of the brush wars scattered throughout the galaxy—some of which are no doubt inspired by the matadorial icon, Khadaji—then they might begin to attend to nits. Until then, all I have to worry about are freelancers trying to score points, or pro-Confed fanatics."

"There seems to be no shortage of them," Dirisha said. She sipped at her cup of hot herb tea.

Carlos flashed his smile at her. "Admittedly so. Still, now I have you to worry about them—"

A soft chime sounded, that of the communicator inset into the wall over the small table. "Yes?" Carlos said.

"We've arrived at the port," came a female voice. "Expect to see us in, oh, an hour or so." The voice was clear and strong, and Dirisha got a mental image of a woman who knew what she was about.

"Good," Carlos said. "I can hardly wait."

He sipped at his citrus juice before answering Dirisha's unspoken question. "Beel," he said, "in charge of the Antag Union's money, such that we have. The brightest woman in the organization, if not this system. And my spouse."

Dirisha's stomach clutched. She gulped at her tea, swallowed too much, and burned her mouth for her trouble. She knew he was contracted, why should hearing that his spouse was arriving make her feel uneasy?

"Beel will have Stenelle and Akeem with her, back from their adventures in galactic geography. I don't get to see as much of them as I'd like." He seemed troubled, but then brightened. "I have holographs of them, would you like to see?"

"Sure," Dirisha said, a weak smile on her lips.

The pictures showed a striking woman with streaked black hair standing in the middle of a pair of teenagers. The boy had red hair, was about thirteen, and the image of Carlos. The girl was perhaps two years older, nearly as tall as her brother, and wore her hair cut in green frizzlocks.

"Very attractive," Dirisha said.

Carlos smiled broadly. "I know."

Dirisha could think of nothing else to say, but the new silence was discomforting, too much so to allow to stand. She said, "The new sensor system has been delivered, I'll get around to testing and installing it today. I wish you'd consider my idea to relocate to a more defensible location, though."

Carlos waved one hand in a half-shrug. "My work is the most important thing, and I can do that best here."

"If my observations are any indication, you work too hard. Sleeping and eating are considered necessary for optimum health." Dirisha's voice was dry.

Carlos laughed. "Funny." He finished his juice and stood. "Shall we get to it?"

Dirisha came to her feet. "Your show, Deuce."

It was some weeks later. Carlos had just entered the *betydelse* space when Dirisha got the call from the perimeter gate.

"Three for the Prebendary," the guard said. "His spouse and offspring. Shall I admit them?"

"Don't be droll," Dirisha said. "Of course."

Dirisha turned, and watched Carlos play the triple communications mode, both hands working quickly. The guard— she still thought of him as Spit-shine—had orders to report anybody seeking an audience with Carlos. He might not like it, but he did as he was told. She wondered what would have happened if she'd told him to turn Carlos's family back. She wondered what kind of a woman Beel Carlos was, that she could command so much obvious respect and affection from her husband. Not to mention mothering his children—

Port entered the room. "Fem Carlos is here."

"Allow her to come in."

She was a fair-sized woman, not as large as Dirisha, but not small. She wore a plain white tunic and pants, and pearl silk slippers. The children were not with her.

Beel Carlos smiled and raised her hand in a palm-out greeting to Dirisha. Dirisha returned the gesture.

"Ah, Fem Zuri. I've heard so much about you! How delightful to meet you at last."

A forthright comment, without any sign of condescension. Dirisha inclined her head slightly. "Fem Carlos."

"Beel, please." She smiled.

"And I'm Dirisha."

Beel looked at her husband. "How is he doing? He looks tired."

"He works too hard," Dirisha said.

Beel turned toward her. "Yes. He thinks he can do it all himself, he doesn't delegate nearly enough. I'm glad you agree. Maybe between the two of us, we can slow him down."

Dirisha's smile came grudgingly, but it came. Beel was concerned about Carlos, it showed in her gestures and in her voice. Dirisha liked her, a gut reaction.

"I thought you had your children with you?"

Beel smiled. "They're in the rec room. They love their father, but they aren't particularly interested in watching him work." She turned back toward Carlos.

But you don't mind, do you? Dirisha watched Beel without seeming to, cataloguing what she saw: a handsome woman, with good muscle tone; she carried herself well; she was obviously bright; she was good-natured. Dirisha could find nothing obvious to dislike.

Damn, why'd I think that? Why should I dislike her? She's my client's mate, and he's nothing special.

But far down a little-used corridor in her mind, something laughed. *Yeah?* it seemed to say. *Who's fooling whom, child? He's special enough.*

Dirisha clamped down on the thought, her attention focused on Carlos again. She had her job, her skills, her self.

That was all she needed, all she had ever needed.

But is it what you want, *child?* came the voice.

On the carefully manicured grounds of the Antag Union's complex, the three of them walked.

Carlos and Beel laughed and talked, strolling arm in arm, while Dirisha scanned the grounds and sky, alert for any possible attacks. She didn't like being in the open like this, but she couldn't force Carlos to stay indoors.

They passed three-hundred-year-old twisted trees, none more than two meters tall, bent into strange shapes, each unique in its design. The grass was a thick mat under their feet, a strain so dark the green seemed almost purple in the midday sunlight. Beel and Carlos laughed, at some private joke, and Dirisha wished she were elsewhere. She had been taught that a good matador became a piece of the furniture; that a client should be able to do or say anything, without worry that his bodyguard would care or condemn; that nothing said or done in the presence of a matador by her client would ever go a step further. Dirisha knew all this, and she was trying to be what she had been trained to be. But she was interested.

"Dirisha?" Beel.

"Yes?"

"Since we are both agreed that Rajeem works entirely too hard, don't you think it would be a good idea if he took a short leave? Got away to some place where he could rest?"

"Hold on a minute here—" Carlos began.

"Hush," Beel cut in. "Dirisha?"

Dirisha couldn't help the smile. "You're right. I think a vacation would be good idea."

"If you two are through deciding my future—"

"We aren't," Beel cut in again. "We'll let you know when we are." To Dirisha, she said, "There is an old estate the Union owns in the Southern Reaches, the perfect place. Off the cast lanes, remote enough so few people even know it exists. A couple of weeks there would do him a world of good."

Dirisha considered it. There might be some security problems, but she could manage those. Part of protecting a client was external, but part of it was in keeping the client from damaging his or her self, if possible. The man was drawn, he needed a break. "Sounds okay," Dirisha said.

"Fems, I don't want to butt in—"

"Then don't," Beel said. "I'll be here for three days before my meeting on Tatsu with the Mitsunashi Group, we'll relax and get you ready; then, you and Dirisha can go to the Perkins' estate. Oh, don't look so petulant, you can take your transceiver and keep in touch with things—as long as Dirisha promises to make you hold it to a minimum."

Carlos grinned, and held his palms out. "What can I say? Two against one, I give up."

Beel laughed, and put an arm around Carlos, hugging him to her. She smiled at Dirisha, and something in her look made Dirisha feel like a co-conspirator, in a plot she didn't quite understand, but was quite happy to go along with.

Despite Beel's comment about resting, Carlos drove himself like a work beast. He arose at dawn, did an hour of kung fu forms, showered, ate breakfast and went to work. He seldom stopped for a midday meal, and worked twelve or fifteen hours at a stretch. He wrote, called, saw visitors, made deals, spoke to groups, gave interviews. He did spend some time with Beel and his children, but only a few moments here and there, an hour at most. He seemed tireless.

Carlos leaped and chopped downward with both hands, snapping his right leg out in a kick, his bare foot extended,

toes curled back. He touched down lightly on the grass, and
jumped into the air again, repeating the snap kick, but thrust-
ing his stiffened fingers into the solar plexus of his imaginary
opponent this time, the backs of his hands together. As he
came down, he pulled his hands apart in a tearing motion.
He landed, lifted his right leg and went into a crane stance,
blocking in a half circle to his right hip with his right hand,
his left held ready to claw. . . .

Dirisha watched the martial dance with a professional
eye, grading Carlos mentally as he moved. He was good.
Not great, but not bad. His motions were clean, mostly, and
his flow even, save for a few small bobbles. The dance was
called "Bear", after a terran carnivore. Many of the fighting
kata were named for animals, real and mythical. Dirisha
didn't know much about bears, but Carlos's motions seemed
shaggy, somehow, and powerful.

Of course, dancing through forms was not altogether an
indication of fighting skill; still, the Ninety-Seven Steps of
sumito didn't seem all that effective as a fighting art, at
first glance. Anyway, Carlos didn't have to worry about
that, now.

He leaped, hands whirring in tight, clawing motions. He
twisted in a half-circle, ducked, and drove one fist into an
invisible groin. . . .

"—results of the intersystem poll show Confed popu-
larity waning in four sectors—"

"—contributions have risen by sixteen percent—"

"—insurrection has broken out on Ago's Moon—

"—cannot transship contraindicated materials—

The voices and holograms filled the air over the net feed
in the information room next to Carlos's office. Dirisha
listened with half her attention, watching Carlos eagerly
absorb the input. He thrived on it, she could see that. His
energy was high, his *ki* focused, and he moved as precisely

in this as he did in his kung fu dances. He loved all this, she saw. Here was a man who got things done, something Dirisha had always admired. He was powerful and self-assured, and his competence drew her, as a Seeker was drawn to a charismatic Sermoner. Taken in pieces, there was no one thing about Carlos that was particularly outstanding; taken as a whole, the man became synergistically attractive.

It had taken some time to arrange the trip, but finally they were on their way. On the hopper to the Southern Reaches, Carlos sat across from Dirisha, staring through the densecris portal at the vast forests over which they passed. Dirisha was working, even as they flew, but there was little she could do directly at the moment. The hopper was as sound as the electromechanics could make it; there was an escort fighter, armed to the wingtips, flying shotgun; the hopper pilot was the best the Antags could find, a woman who could put the craft close enough to a ditch to net minnows without getting the hull damp, according to her stats. Port and Starboard were already at the estate, with a sweep-team.

"Do you really think this is a good idea?" Carlos said, interrupting Dirisha's mental catalogue of precautions.

"Yes. Beel is looking out for you. You're an important man to a lot of people, Rajeem. It isn't just the work you can do personally, you're part of something larger. A symbol. Like Khadaji."

"I doubt if I'm in that class, thank you."

Dirisha shifted in her seat. "Maybe, maybe not. I don't have Pen's long view, I'm more a here-and-now person. But if you don't take care of yourself, you won't be either a symbol or able to do the work. Simple."

He nodded. "Sensible." He turned his gaze back to the forest eight kilometers below.

Dirisha looked away, feeling pleased. The man was not stupid. He accepted the need to take care of himself without false modesty. More, he had asked her opinion as if he really cared what she thought. Pen had taught her that clients would come to trust matadors, to lean on them. That was part of his grand plan too, whatever it was. Still, Dirisha liked hearing Carlos ask, liked having him pay attention to what she said, as if she were one of his important connections, with something valid to give him. It made her feel needed. And warm. And, yet, it bothered her. She was a professional, doing a job she had been trained to do for years. She should be able to do it objectively. . . . A memory flowed then, of Pen talking about objectivity versus subjectivity. What had he said? That a person couldn't be truly objective about important things? She hadn't understood it then, and she wasn't sure she understood it now, but something about it danced at the hidden corners of her mind, capering like some demented sufi. She only caught a glimpse of it, and what she saw, she didn't like. The thing pranced and pointed a finger at her. *Puppet,* it said gleefully.

Puppet.

TWENTY ─────────────

Dirisha watched Carlos work the *betydelse* space, amazed again at two things: him, and her perceptions of him. After all the years of working the Flex, of training to become a matador, with all the drilling, she still underestimated people. She'd expected Carlos to be a stuffed-tunic politico, a religious fanatic, a man concerned with things somehow unworldly; a man with a mission, but without means to achieve it on his own. Sister, had she been wrong.

In the *betydelse* space, Carlos waved his right hand in a series of quick, short gestures. Programming mode signals, she knew, though she couldn't read them. Until recently, she hadn't known that much. At the same time, Carlos fluttered his left hand back and forth, wiggling his fingers in a precise pattern. Mathematical code. And, while both hands spoke separate languages to the transmitter, he sub-vocalized yet a third set of instructions to the machine. It was like watching a master musician playing some esoteric instrument, made all the more impressive by knowing how complex the tune must be, even though she was unable to hear or understand it.

Dirisha raised her left hand to her chest and caught the chunk of black plastic hanging from her neck by a thin strap. She touched one of the controls, and a miniature hologram appeared over the small module, a single word: CLEAR.

Dirisha released the mod. A hundred sensors spread over the estate were her eyes and ears, and they saw and heard nothing dangerous to her charge. That didn't mean she could relax, she'd learned that lesson well enough; still, it did mean it was unlikely an assassin skulked the grounds, wait-ing for his, her or its chance to kill.

She turned back to watch Carlos. Rajeem, as he kept telling her to call him. An amazing man. Strong, quick, bright and caring, Rajeem Carlos impressed Dirisha as no man had impressed her before—not Khadaji, not Pen, no one.

With a quick flourish, Carlos finished his triple-command performance in the *betydelse* space. The glowing air around him dimmed as he stepped away from the reader and into the ordinariness of the room. He blinked, coming from the trance, and saw Dirisha. He smiled at her.

Dirisha's heart leaped, and she felt that irrational flow of joy again, at somehow pleasing him.

"I didn't hear you come in," he said.

"Good. That'd mean I was losing my touch." She re-turned his smile.

For a moment, they stood there, smiling at each other like idiots. Carlos broke the locked stare by shaking his head. "There's so much to do, Dirisha. I have a dozen things

I should be attending to, people to see, information to process—"

"Hey," she said, "the reason we came here is for you to rest, remember? You can't do it all by yourself."

His face lost the serious look after a moment, and he smiled again. "You're right." He took two steps toward her, put his arm around her shoulders, and urged her toward the veranda. "What shall we do to rest?"

Dirisha was very much aware of the warmth of his arm touching her, even through the orthoskins she wore. Of the muscle tone of that arm, of its hardness and power—Chang, she had to stop this! He was a client, he should be nothing more, no matter how attractive he was. Besides, he was a man with a destiny involving worlds, involving maybe the galaxy. All she was was a well-trained bodyguard. But she couldn't deny how she felt. Rajeem Carlos pulled at her, a pull she had no defense against, despite all her skills. Stupid, Deuce, stupid. He doesn't think of you that way, he's contracted, he has children, he has his work, so don't travel that lane.

On the veranda, Carlos dropped his arm and stretched, taking in the lush greenery that came almost to the edge of the stone patio. The air was fresh, full of oxy and evergreen scents, and the sun had removed the night's chill without overheating the morning. It was a beautiful place, made more so, Dirisha thought, in that she and Carlos were alone in it; Port and Starboard patrolled the perimeter, along with other guards, klicks away from the main lodge.

"Do you know about this place?" he asked.

Dirisha knew what the background sphere had told her, but she shook her head. Let him tell it.

"The estate belonged to the Perkins family. Originally, it was a hunting preserve. No-kill, of course. The house was a lodge, you can see how rustic it still is. The family would come here on outings, they would stalk the whelves

and demi-trogs with tranquil darts, then come back here for
rest and relaxation. At one time, the gardens here were
considered the finest on-planet." He waved one arm, to
encompass the estate. "Would you like to walk? There are
some beautiful paths, so I'm told."

Dirisha nodded. She had seen the paths, while setting
her sensors. They were beautiful, even where the flowers
had gone wild and the underbrush had begun to encroach
on the once carefully-tended grounds.

They walked. The pathways were laid out in gentle curves,
winding among the trees and bushes so that a viewer could
behold as much of the beauty as possible even on a short
trip.

Dirisha was more interested in watching Carlos than in
the scenery. For the first time in months, he seemed to relax.
The lines of tension in his face smoothed a little, his shoulders sagged from their normally tight set. It made her feel
good to see it; at the same time, Dirisha felt that tiny stab
of fear that she could care so much. Ah, this was why she
could never let it go. It was why she had never been able
to relax fully with a lover, not even Geneva. It would mean
being naked emotionally, being vulnerable. It would mean
taking a risk, to trust somebody that much. She didn't know
if she could do that, not after all the years of holding to
herself. Her greatest strength, Mayli Wu had said. And her
greatest weakness. She could see that, now. But she couldn't
see how to get past it—

Something rustled the flowery bush just ahead and to
their right. Instantly, Dirisha stepped ahead of Carlos and
blocked his body with her own. Her right spetsdöd came
up, an automatic motion, to point at the bush.

"Come out careful, Deuce, or spend the next six months
locked!"

A small creature with long ears darted across the path,

and Dirisha tracked it with her spetsdöd. She held her fire
at the last instant.

Behind her, Carlos laughed.

She turned to face him.

"A rabbit," he said. "Or the local version of it. A her-
bivore, and harmless."

Dirisha raised from her crouch. Her sensors were designed to pick up anything massing more than ten kilos
moving around in the brush, so that explained why the robit,
or whatever he'd called it, didn't register. Well, okay, it
was harmless, but she didn't know that, the background
sphere hadn't said anything about small animals running
wild—

"Thank you," Carlos said, his face grave.

"For what?" She was puzzled. "It wasn't a threat."

Carlos stepped closer to her, so that they were nearly
touching. "It could have been. You were willing to let it
take you rather than me."

Dirisha looked up at his face. Tall as she was, Carlos
was half a head taller. And he probably had twenty kilos
on her, he was a big man. Not as big as Bork, but big. "It's
my job, Rajeem."

He raised his hands and touched her shoulders, sliding
his palms down to her arms. "Yes."

What Dirisha saw in his face then was desire. He *wanted*
her, as she wanted him. Was it only sex? Spurred by the
imagined danger they'd just faced? Or was it more?

He leaned down and kissed her. Softly, gently, a press
and joining of parted lips, so tender there was almost no
sensation of physically touching him. But there was no
mistaking the feeling of being joined. Dirisha had read and
seen stories all of her life of the electric jolt that passed
between lovers, but she had never felt it. Until now.

He pulled away, to look at her.

She had seen the look before, she realized. Bork had worn it, after Mayli Wu had asked him to kiss her. After that kiss, Bork had looked at Mayli just like Carlos looked at her now. It shocked her into a stunned silence.

Dirisha sucked in a quick breath, and felt her pulse quicken. He called to her, his essence called to hers, and all the days past of feeling drawn to him came to this moment—he wanted her, as well. Had it been that way all along? She had wanted him from the beginning though she refused it, never thinking or hoping he might feel the same way.

The lifetime of a god passed. Dirisha grew from a child to a woman in that time, her life formed a parade past her stunned gaze, showing her herself, as she had been, as she was, as she might be. Multiple paths lay before her, and she had to choose which one she would walk. From the depths of her mind a small thought spiraled up, a tiny thing which had lain buried for so long it almost could not free itself. She watched it idly as the thought rose, and was shattered as she understood what it meant: she didn't have to give up anything, she would lose no part of herself if she gave in and loved this man, let him love her. *You'll be more, not less!* But how could it happen? She was a matadora, supposed to protect her client, no more.

She could almost hear Pen laughing as she understood finally what it was he had done, what she had so stupidly failed to see before: he had set her up, just as he had set Geneva up. Pen, the cosmic matchmaker!

Why? Was it just to make sure Rajeem Carlos got the best bodyguard possible, according to Pen's theory of subjective/objective? Or was there more? Had he been trying to complete something lacking in her, as he had done in Geneva? Damn him! Did he think he was a god, to twist people to his whims? Dammit, she didn't have to do it his way! She could turn and walk! But. . . .

But. Dirisha felt it within her, the desire for Carlos, something beyond simple sex, beyond wanting to do a good job. It was powerful, the attraction, the most powerful thing she had felt in years, an emotion which gripped her like steel clamps and refused to let go, even though she knew she had been led to it like one blind. The word was slow in coming, and it didn't feel as she had always thought it would, but it came: love. More powerful than fanaticism, Pen had said. Dirisha knew it was true; it would not be denied.

A microsecond, a god's lifetime, the space of it passed, leaving behind the realization. Her greatest strength was her greatest weakness, Mayli had said. And once she realized it, it was no more. Dirisha cast away her fear of losing herself, along with her anger at Pen, with as little effort as smiling.

She watched Rajeem see it, saw his face light with an answering glow, as he bent to kiss her again.

Dirisha put her arms around his neck, and the kiss flowered with passion. Suddenly she wanted this man, like she had never wanted another. His hands stroked her back and buttocks, urging her to him, and she pressed against his body as though trying to fuse into it.

His lips and tongue moved against her neck. Dirisha laughed into the air of the forest. Rajeem moved lower, tugging at her clothes. He untabbed her tunic, pulled her pants down, and bent to kiss her breasts, her belly, her mons. She felt his flickering tongue dart against her clitoris, followed by his lips, sucking her inner labia gently. Ah, yes! Her knees trembled, but she continued to stand, moving her fingers in his hair as he kissed her. He held her buttocks with one hand and pulled her against his face. She knew she couldn't let go, it was too dangerous out here, and even through the passion, she was aware of her surroundings. She allowed him to continue for awhile more, then urged him to stand again. "Wait," she said. She repeated his earlier actions, sliding down his body. She opened his pants, and took his penis into her mouth. She moved on him, lips and tongue working. He groaned again, and bent to catch her under the arms. He lifted her, as easily, it seemed to Dirisha, as a man lifting a child. He cupped her buttocks with both hands and raised her until her chin was over his head. Then, slowly and carefully, he lowered her, entering her until they were joined in that most ancient of man and woman connections. He began to thrust, holding her, and she in turn thrust against him.

She thought he would fall when he came, and he shook, but held his stance. She could feel him pulsing within her, and she kissed his neck and hugged him, wanting to keep him inside her forever. He stood that way for a long time.

After a while, Dirisha laughed.

"What?"

She leaned back so she could see his face. "Pen," she said. "He knew this would happen. That you and I would find each other, that we would get to this point." Then she laughed again. It didn't matter. She would kiss him and thank him for his twisted machinations the next time she saw him. The son of a bezelwart. She loved him.

Carlos laughed, too. "Yes, he and Beel would probably get along fine."

Dirisha felt a stab of something in her gut. Fear? What would Beel think? What kind of relationship did they have, was it monogamous?

Carlos said, "Yes, indeed. With all the pillow-plumping she was doing, she'll be most pleased."

Dirisha leaned back, still joined to Carlos at the pubis. "What?"

"Why do you think she sent us off here together, alone? She knows me, and she likes you—a lot. I could tell that the first time you two met." He squeezed her buttocks, still grinning widely. "You have anything against women lovers? Or triads?"

"No."

"Good. I have a feeling you and I and Beel are going to get along just fine."

Still riding his hips, Dirisha smiled. "What say we go inside? It'd be a lot easier for me to relax without having to worry about something coming out of the bushes while your mad tongue works." She was amazed at herself. Pen was right, once again. She was no less a pro now than she had been before. Objectivity? Subjectivity? Words, they didn't mean anything. Her skills hadn't disappeared because she unbound a part of herself which had been strapped down tightly all of her life.

"Anything you say." He began to walk, carrying Dirisha still wrapped around him.

She laughed, and knew how it was going to be.

It was going to be great.

TWENTY-ONE ————————

CARLOS WAS STILL asleep as Dirisha arose nude from the
bed. She grinned at him and walked quietly away, into the
communications room. Dawn was beginning, faint and
feathery blue light came through the window as Dirisha
padded toward the security com board. The sensors were
silent. The night team's in-checks were identical: no sus-
picious activity.

Dirisha kneeled on the backless orthopedic form and
stroked the external communications module into glowing
life. She had a message she wanted to send. To Geneva.

The computer blinked and lit the air.

READY TO TRANSMIT. ACCESS CODE?

Geneva was on Earth by now, protecting an ambassador.
Dirisha didn't know those codes, but she did know how to
send to Matador Villa. Pen would get the message to

Geneva. Dirisha didn't doubt that he was expecting her to call.

There were a million things she could say, but they weren't necessary, the essence could be distilled to a few simple lines. She punched in the access code for Pen at the Villa, but rather than type the words of the message itself, Dirisha wanted to say it aloud. "This is for Geneva, Pen. But I want to say something to you, too: Thanks. It took me a while, but I got it.

"Hi, Brat. I know I'm slow to catch on sometimes, but even though you're light years away, you need to know I've finally figured it out. I love you, Geneva. It took somebody else to show me how locked up I've been all my life, and I love him, too, but I've discovered that love isn't limited that way. So you take care until I can tell it to you in person."

Dirisha smiled at the computer, and used her hands to close the communication.

ACKNOWLEDGED, the computer flashed. HARD COPY?

"Negative," Dirisha said. She didn't need to see it.

Carlos came into the room behind her, Dirisha heard his soft footfalls on the spunsilk carpet. He came to stand behind her, and slid his hand over her shoulders to cup her bare breasts.

"Morning, Rish. What's up?" He yawned.

She twisted to look up at him. "Taking care of some old business," she said. "Making a couple of connections clear."

"Um. Good. What about coming back to bed? I have a connection you might like."

"Yeah?"

"Well. You won't know unless you try it."

"How can I resist such brilliant logic?"

Carlos bent and kissed her on the neck.

*   *   *

Dirisha was staring happily at Carlos's tousled red hair when the bedroom communicator chimed.

"Yes?" Carlos said.

"Good day, husband," came Beel's voice. The holoproj screen lit with her face, smiling. "Got something against visual this morning?"

Carlos glanced at Dirisha next to him in the bed. She smiled and shook her head. Carlos said, "Visual on."

Beel's face broke into a wide grin as she saw Carlos and Dirisha together. Dirisha sat up, and the sheet fell to her waist, to reveal her nudity.

"Oh, my," Beel said, her voice filled with mock horror.

Carlos laughed. "Shit. Now tell me it never crossed your mind."

Beel tried to keep a straight face. "Why, it never crossed my mind—" then she began to laugh. When she finished, she said, "I gather you've been able to keep him from working too hard, Dirisha?"

"We've been relaxing some, yes."

"Good. I've finished my business offworld. The children are back in school; would you two mind company?"

Carlos looked at Dirisha again; she smiled. He turned back toward the screen. "We'd love company, especially yours."

"I'll see you this evening, then."

After the communication ended, Dirisha said, "Just to satisfy my curiosity, do you two do this often?"

"No. We're particular whom we share each other with. You are very special, Dirisha. There are few people I feel safe or comfortable with, fewer still I can trust and love. It's the same with Beel. We're stingy with ourselves, and with our time. It's too valuable to waste on just anybody."

"Thank you," Dirisha said, bending to kiss his shoulder.

"Oh, you can do better than that!"

He giggled, and Dirisha kissed him again. It wasn't so awful, being able to let go with somebody. How could she have ever been afraid of it? Pen had been—as usual, dammit—right. She understood fully now what he had meant when he's said that Geneva could give the galaxy a run for its money for somebody she loved. There was a new dimension Dirisha had never seen before, and it was a good place to be. Too, she understood something about Pen which she had wondered about: he treated his students differently. Not everyone would get what she had gotten, for not everyone had her particular strengths and weaknesses. Like a man raising unique and exotic plants, Pen watered and fed each one what he thought best to allow it to grow properly. For her, it had been love, as it had with Geneva. For others, it might be something quite different. She shook her head. Ah, what a master gardener he was. . . .

Starboard and Dirisha stood on the veranda behind the lodge. A thunderstorm was building to the west; thick, gray cumulonimbus clouds stacked and darkened, and lightning forked among them. Dirisha counted the seconds, and listened for thunder. The rumble came, and she judged the storm to be about twenty klicks away. It wouldn't be long before it arrived. She turned away from the approaching rain and back toward Starboard. "Tell me again," she said.

"They seemed just a pair of kids looking for a place to play dork-and-bush, like they hinted. Attractive couple. They were on an old flitter with local tags. I checked out the code and the flitter was registered in the name he gave me. I ran a background and the coolfile says he's a local boy, works in an agrocommune, a plant tech. I didn't see any sub-rosa gear, and my weapons' scanners came up empty."

Dirisha nodded. So far, nobody else had approached the estate in the week she and Carlos had been here. Beel was due up in a hour or so, but that was Beel.

"It's only fifteen klicks to the agrocommune," Dirisha said. "Not too far a trip if you're looking for privacy outside. There were signs of people who'd sneaked in before you arrived, right? Beer containers, picnic trash?"

Starboard chewed at his lower lip. "Yeah."

"But something doesn't feel right?"

He nodded. "Yeah. I dunno what, nothing I can finger, but something. I wish I'd had an electropophy set-up at the gate. I'd have felt a lot better if I could have shined a truth-sucker at the kid."

Dirisha considered what to do. It probably meant nothing; on the other hand, a good matadora covered all her bets all the time. "Tell you what," she said, "you get one of the night-crew to cover for you and go check it out. Talk to the local cools at the commune, verify the boy's story. Find out about the girl. You can pick up some supplies while you're there. That make you feel better about it?"

"Yeah, it would."

"Go. Take the big aircar."

Starboard walked away, and Dirisha looked back at the distant clouds. The bottoms were almost purple now, and she could see the rain slanting in a dark gray wall to the ground. A cool wind blew over her, stirring the bonsai trees and flowers. Definitely coming this way, that storm. The spaces between the lightning and thunder grew shorter. There was a smell of anticipation in the air, positive ions stirring. The rain would play hell with her sensor system, even with full-filters running. She'd have to tune them down so low they'd only be marginally effective. The confounder detectors would be useless. She didn't like it. The only remedy was to field more of the crew, and making them stand out in a driving downpour wouldn't gain her any points, but it couldn't be helped. They'd grumble that it was a waste of time; that it would be highly unlikely anybody could pass the fence-field or gate on foot, that only a moron would fly in a thunderstorm. They'd be right, too, but Dirisha had been trained too well to slack off because something was "highly unlikely." "Highly unlikely" could get you and your client dead. And "impossible" was hard to come by. Better to cover it and be safe.

Beel arrived at the gate just after the storm opened up over the lodge. The constant patter of the rain nearly drowned the voice of the guard as he called Dirisha.

"—Fem Carlos, alone, rental aircar," the guard said.

"Don't keep her waiting," Dirisha said.

She broke the connection and turned to Carlos, who stood staring out at the rain. A gust of wind shook the lodge. Lightning flashed, and the thunder followed it almost immediately. Close. The lodge was faraday-shielded, so there was no danger from a direct strike, but a tree could fall on the building if enough wind or juice worked on it.

Dirisha went to stand next to Carlos. He slipped one arm around her waist, and cupped her hip. "I love to watch it storm," he said. "When I was a child on Earth, we lived in a semi-tropical region where there were a lot of electrical storms, especially in the summer. Sometimes I'd stand outside, under the overhang of a roof or with an umbrelfield, and just soak up the power I could feel."

"You weren't afraid of the lightning?"

"No. Too stupid for that. I thought I was invulnerable, that I'd live forever." He turned away from the window and smiled at Dirisha.

"Beel is here. The gate guard just called."

Carlos slipped his other arm around Dirisha and drew her close. "Good. I think you'll really like her."

Dirisha put her hands on Carlos's back and rubbed gently. "I already like her, Rajeem. She gave me a pretty good present this week."

"Only 'pretty good?' I'm crushed."

"Yeah, you look crushed, all right. It was terrific, and you know it."

"Well," he said, "you aren't too bad yourself. For a woman who could tie me up in knots, if she wanted."

"Better watch it, I just might. I don't want to get out of practice."

The entry admit sang, a humming tone. "Oops, company."

"Great timing, my spouse. I'll get it—"

"You stay right here," Dirisha ordered. "We both know it's Beel, but you pay me to be sure."

Carlos inclined his head a fraction. "Your show, Deuce," he said. His voice was a fair imitation of Dirisha's.

She laughed. "A mimic. Is there no end to your talent?"

Carlos turned back to stare out at the storm, and Dirisha walked to the entrance. The doorway was in the lee of the building and there was a broad overhang over the porch, but the wind was wild enough to spray the area with mist. The camera lens mounted over the door picked up the image at the door and channeled it to a holoproj inset next to the electronic lock panel. Beel, sure enough, and wet. Her rental vehicle sat only ten yards away on the lawn, but there were puddles like small ponds between the car and the lodge, and the rain churned these into rippling sheets.

Dirisha opened the door. Beel ran into the foyer.

"Great Holy Chang," Beel said, "I thought I was going to drown!"

Dirisha helped her remove her sodden overcloak. Beel bent to tug her dotic boots off; she tossed them into the corner with a *clump,* then turned back to Dirisha. "Hi," she said. She extended her arms, and the two women hugged warmly. There was no awkwardness for Dirisha, only a feeling of comfort and acceptance. After a moment, they released the embrace. Beel leaned back a little. "You look great," she said.

"I feel it. Thanks, Beel. For—for . . . all—"

Beel clasped both of Dirisha's hands with hers. "You're welcome."

The two exchanged grins. Finally, Dirisha said, "Rajeem is in the main room—"

"—staring out at the storm," Beel finished.

"Come on." Holding hands, Dirisha led Beel down the hallway.

Carlos turned and smiled when he saw them. "There is truly a Nirvana," he said. "I have passed into it, for certain." He spread his arms wide, to encompass both women. The three formed a human triangle in front of the window.

Dirisha had never felt so loved and protected before. She began to cry silently, the tears running down her face to soak into the clothes of these two most wonderful people.

Love, but not blind love, not the hyped romantic love of the holoproj fictions. Even as they waited for her, Dirisha did her security checks, and took the time to do it right. A full electronic scan, a quick basetouch with the guards. Now she could relax better. Maybe not totally, but as much as was possible for a matadora. Ah, Pen. I love you, too. For what you have given me.

When she had worked as a trull years past, Dirisha had sometimes been in a sexual triad with clients who wished it. It had felt awkward then; it did not feel awkward now. It was simply *more*—more hands, more lips, more of everything. It was all quite natural: that she should stroke a female breast while kissing a male one; that she should have a male organ inside her while touching a female mons. No one was in a hurry, no one was playing sexual power games, no one wanted anything except to express love and to give pleasure.

Dirisha had never felt anything like it; it was a peak experience, as the first time with Rajeem Carlos alone had been. Not simply sexual, it was due to what lay behind it: love. Mayli Wu had been right.

Hands and lips and breasts and all the rest flowered and touched and stroked. Dirisha's orgasm stretched like gold and broke gently, snapping her into bliss. She came again, and again, another new experience, and the night flowed like chilled honey, going on forever.

"I love you," she said. And heard twin echoes in the warm darkness which enwrapped them. The rain on the roof continued. It was the sound which lulled Dirisha into contented sleep.

TWENTY-TWO ———————

IN THE MORNING, it was still raining. Dirisha slipped from the big bed, leaving Beel and Rajeem wrapped together, and went to do her job.

The weathercast was succinct. Yesterday's storm was merely the leading one on a front. It would likely rain for the next two days. Dirisha smiled. Somehow, the idea of being cooped in the lodge with Beel and Rajeem didn't distress her in the least. The crew outside might hate it, but they were well-paid pros, they'd stand it.

A quick check of her estate sensor gear showed Dirisha what she'd feared had happened. About half of the equipment failed to register on her board. Probably a lot of the spikes were underwater, and between that and the electrical activity, it was a wonder any of them were operational. Well. When it dried up, they could be replaced.

The communicator cheeped, announcing an incoming call.

"Zuri here."

Starboard's voice came from the instrument. "Dirisha. I got stuck in the commune when the storm hit. A tree blew down on the road."

"I got a notation on that," Dirisha said. "Port logged in your earlier call."

"Yeah, well, he didn't log in what I dug up last night. We might have a problem."

Dirisha felt a sudden chill, and she fought to suppress an epinephrinic surge. She cupped her hands over her *hara* point and did a centering *reiki*. "Let's hear it."

"The boy in the flitter came up status-clear. Local kid, no history of trouble, average/normal. I came up deadscreen on the girl with him. Nobody knows her. Worse, the boy— his name is Ashir—hasn't been around since I saw him. His dorm-cube shows he didn't sleep there last shift."

Dirisha considered it. "Could be he and the girl got caught in the storm, decided to sleep in the car."

"Yeah, maybe." Starboard sounded doubtful.

"Something else is bothering you."

There was a short pause, as if Starboard were gathering his thoughts. "Things are pretty loose here, as far as security goes, nobody keeps indexes on comings and goings. But nobody I've talked to knows the girl Ashir was with. I gave out a good description and got null on her. This is a small place, maybe a thousand people, long-timers, mostly. Somebody ought to be able to place her."

"So she's not a local," Dirisha said.

"Yeah. Then where'd she come from? This is the only civilization for a couple hundred klicks in any direction. Seems strange that our boy Ashir would come up with an out-communer and then just happen to flit out to the estate. It just doesn't *feel* right."

Dirisha took a deep breath and released it. Instinct was what Starboard was talking about, gut-level feeling that defied rational explanation. Dirisha had seen it often enough to pay attention to it, especially when the person having it was trained in one of the Arts. Starboard's reaction to the mystery woman triggered an uneasiness in Dirisha: something was wrong, and both she and Starboard felt it without having a logical reason. Zen-trouble, and enough to cause caution. She said, "Okay, I copy your feeling. I'd rather have you here than there; as soon as the road is clear, flit back to the estate."

"Copy that, Dirisha. Clear."

Dirisha turned away from the com. It might mean nothing; then again, it might mean a lot. With half her security gear inoperative, she felt vulnerable. Maybe this trip hadn't been such a good idea.

She smiled at that. No, the idea was good. And what had happened so far was better than good. Only she couldn't afford to get slack, just because she'd discovered a Great Truth. People could get hurt that way. Rajeem, maybe. That wasn't a pleasant thought at all.

Breakfast was a happy affair. Rajeem and Beel both glowed, and Dirisha felt as if she also shined with an internal fire. They were so relaxed, and so comfortable to be around. Rajeem cooked the meal—it was well-prepared, a mix of exotic cake-bread, fruits and tofu steaks—and everything tasted wonderful. Dirisha couldn't remember feeling so relaxed before.

Starboard's call broke the mood, and Dirisha's comfort. Dirisha smiled as she answered the com, but the smile faded quickly.

"The local cools found Ashir's flitter, a few klicks away. Burned up. The rain kept the fire from spreading, but it was enough to kick in the forestry station's smoke detectors.

Ashir was in the wreck, dead, but the rain apparently kept him from roasting too bad. One of the cools was a medic, he says the kid didn't die accidentally."

"How?" Dirisha broke in.

"Looks like a slap-cap, back of the head. No sign of the girl."

Suddenly the unknown woman became a real threat. Somebody had killed a local boy, a boy who had driven to the gate of the estate earlier, looking for . . . what? A way in?

"You get back here, stat," she said.

Behind her, Beel laughed at something Rajeem said. Dirisha tuned them out. She punched an all-report code into her operative caster, a simple key-in-to-show-you're-awake command. There were fourteen ops in the field, six off-duty, counting Starboard. Within thirty seconds, seventeen diodes lit on her control board. Starboard was out of range, that left two. Where the hell were they—? Another green dot blinked on. Dirisha coded that one and called him. "Where were you, Tam?"

"Sorry," the voice came back, "I was—ah—answering the call of nature. Had to shake it."

"Next time you take more than thirty seconds to answer *my* call you aren't going to need to shake it anymore, because it will be gone!"

Dirisha looked back at the board. One light stayed dark. She coded in Treacher's number. Nothing. She did a voice-all call. "Anybody seen Treacher? She's not answering."

Nobody had seen her. And Treacher was the gate guard. Oh, shit!

"Marz and Lusso, get to the main gate, stat. The rest of you pair-link and get to your intruder stations. We may have a breach! Move!"

The rain pounded steadily, and the sound of Dirisha's

excitement must have communicated itself to Rajeem and Beel.

"Dirisha?" Rajeem began. "Is something wrong?"

"I'm not sure," she said tightly. "One of my guards isn't answering her call."

"Maybe the rain—" Beel started.

"Maybe," Dirisha cut her off. "But let's not make any dangerous bets. You two see if you can dig up an umbrel-field or three, just in case we need to go out."

"Go out?" Beel said.

Dirisha said, "If somebody dangerous is on the estate, they'll be coming for the lodge. Better for you to be else-where, that happens."

"But surely with all the guards, that isn't likely?"

The com came to life. One of the pair of guards she'd sent to the gate called in. Marz, and he was yelling. "Treacher is unconscious, looks like she's taken the blast of a hand wand at close range! What'll we do?"

"Put an aid kit on her and set up a field of fire to cover yourselves and the gate. Starboard is coming by car. Make sure it's him and let him pass. Spetsdöd anybody else you see. If they're wearing armor, don't get fancy. Use your Parkers."

There was a bright green flash and a sizzle, as the curtain outlining the window behind Beel burst into flame.

"Move!" Dirisha yelled. She jumped up, ran three steps to Beel, and shouldered her away from the window.

Another flash rent the air, melting a hole through the glass window and splashing against the far wall. The wood took fire and began to smoke.

"They've got a charged-particle spitter!" Dirisha yelled. The matadora in her took full control. "Stay down and follow me," she ordered.

Rajeem nodded and began crawling in a military elbow-drag. Beel looked at him. "Do what she says, Beel, she knows what she's doing."

The three of them made it into one of the unused bed-rooms. Dirisha shut the door. Greenish light shined briefly under the door again. Dirisha ran to the window and looked out. They were on the opposite side of the house from the ceepee spitter. The wind had slackened some, but the rain continued to pour unabated. Aside from a few of the bonsai trees twenty or more meters from the house, there was no cover. Dirisha didn't see anybody watching this side of the lodge. They could exit by the window and get to Beel's flitter, since view of the vehicle was blocked from the other side, where the shooter was. But—how many of them were there?

Smoke began to ooze under the closed door. The lodge was on fire from the particle beams. Not much time to think.

"We're going out," Dirisha said. "I'll go first. If some-body shoots me, stay put, otherwise, move fast and drop flat, next to the house, you copy?"

Both of them did.

Dirisha took a deep breath and shoved the spring window wide. She dived out, did a forward roll, and came up into a squat, her spetsdöds pointing at forty-five degree angles from her body.

Nothing, just the rain.

Rajeem followed; Beel was right behind him.

The only sounds Dirisha heard were water dripping from the roof and background wind and rain. "Stay behind me, but close," she said. She began to edge along the side of the lodge. Water splashed from her orthoskins, but she ig-nored it.

At the corner, Dirisha lay flat on the muddy ground and peered around, her face at ankle level. The front of the house looked clear. Could they make it to the flitter? It was only a few meters away, maybe fifteen. A flitter's thincris

and plastic were no protection from a military ceepee weapon,
but if they could clear the lodge area, they would have a
better chance. Why weren't there any other attackers covering the front? Could it be there was only the one, the
woman? Some freelance out to make a name for herself?
If that was the case, Dirisha could have Rajeem and Beel
a klick away in a minute or less.

A big aircar fanned around the bend in the approach
road, rotors churning up thick mists around itself. Dirisha
recognized the vehicle and the driver: Starboard. He must
have seen another flash from the particle weapon, for he
veered to the right, tilting the car and spraying water to the
side.

A green spear lanced at the car, but missed. Starboard
tried to zig-zag, but the aircar was not designed for wheeled
response. The second beam splashed against the car, on the
passenger side. The flitter slowed, and spun. Starboard leaped
out, hit the ground, and started rolling. A third ray ate into
the flitter, and the car exploded, showering plastic and metal
shrapnel against the lodge. A smoking bit of plastic fell a
meter in front of Dirisha. She couldn't see Starboard for
the smoke. That same smoke would obscure the approach
to Beel's flitter. Dirisha rose to a crouch, and started to
wave Rajeem and Beel to follow her.

She stopped. It felt wrong. Whoever was wielding the
ceepee was no amateur. Even if it were only a single woman,
she was too good to start blasting at something as big as
the lodge, hoping to hit her target. No, Dirisha didn't buy
it. She turned toward Beel. "Do you have a remote for your
flitter? A prewarm starter?"

"Y–yes," Beel said, her voice high. "I–in my personal
bag. In the bedroom. Why?"

"I'll tell you later. Look, I want you two to stay right
here. I'll be back in a minute."

"Dirisha—?" Rajeem began.

"It's all right. Just sit tight." She managed a grin, to reassure them.

She went back into the lodge, and opened the door of the bedroom. Black smoke poured in, and Dirisha dropped to the floor. The air was hot and smoky, but breathable. She crawled into the main bedroom and, after scrabbling around a minute, found Beel's bag. She didn't try to find the remote, but went quickly back the way she'd come.

When she returned, Rajeem and Beel looked at Dirisha with questions in their faces. Dirisha found the remote. She peeped around the corner, then pulled her head back and touched the control to start the filter's engine.

A bright flash lit the rain, followed by a boom that pounded on their ears. She dropped the control and looked around the corner once again.

Where Beel's rental flitter had been, there was a smoldering crater in the ground.

Dirisha nodded to herself. "That's what I figured," she said softly. "Stick here," she said. "It's time to end this."

She circled the lodge quickly. She was in time to see a single figure holding a bulky ceepee projector walk carefully through the rain toward the front of the lodge. Dirisha waited until she was sure the assassin was alone, then followed quickly. Dirisha saw Starboard, lying unmoving in the rain.

The woman with the particle weapon moved toward the pit where the flitter had been. Dirisha scooted up behind her, until she was only ten meters away. The woman wore shiftsuit gear, but no armor. The shiftsuit tried to mimic the rain hitting it, but it had not been designed for such, and only looked a puddly-gray.

Dirisha raised her left spetsdöd slowly. She fixed her gaze on the back of the woman's neck, where a centimeter-wide strip of bare flesh was exposed between her hood and jacket. "That's it for you, Sister," Dirisha whispered. And shot.

The woman crumpled, stiffening as she fell. Shock-tox wasn't pleasant, but at least she would be alive, more than she'd intended for her victims.

TWENTY-THREE ─────

"HOW'S GRANDLE?" RAJEEM asked. For a second, Dirisha couldn't place the name; then she remembered. Starboard. She'd been calling the two men by their nicknames, and hadn't thought of them any other way. "Fine. He's got a couple of broken ribs and a liver contusion, and a lump on his head. The medics say he'll be fit in a few days."

They were back at the Antag Union's headquarters, in Rajeem's office. Beel now had her own guard—Port's brother, as it happened—and was busy speaking to some corporate financial seminar. The incident at the country estate had shaken, but hadn't slowed her.

"What about the woman?"

"The medics are still . . . treating her." That was true enough, only there wasn't anything physically wrong with the would-be assassin. She was being "debriefed", a euphemistic term for mind-laundry. She would be turned over to the impatient Confed authorities shortly, but not until Dirisha was satisfied with her. Someone who pointed a deadly weapon at a client was considered to have lost considerable civil rights. Let the Confed stew; the woman was going to be squeezed like a sponge before they got her.

"I was just going to go see how she was doing," Dirisha said.

"Um. I should get back to work," Rajeem said. "Take care, Rish."

The Antag Union's chief psychomed was a tall, muscular man of about forty. He had a lot of smile lines, and his *ki* was strong as he spoke. Dirisha leaned against the wall of his spare office, and listened.

"—surface reactions, of course, and there's no doubt that she killed the boy and tried to kill Pr. Carlos. But unless you're willing to see her as a brain-scrambled turnip, we won't get anything deeper. She's blocked against a scan, psychochem doesn't work, and electropophy deep-probe comes up with nursery rhymes."

Dirisha scratched at her forehead with the barrel of her left spetsdöd. "I don't think it'll be necessary to melt her mind. She's Confed."

The medic looked surprised, but nodded in agreement. "My thought, exactly. Nobody goes to that much trouble to hide something unless it's important. She was carrying neurotoxin, did you know? Under her nails, in a cervical pellet, and behind one ear. If we hadn't been thorough before she came out of the shock-tox, she could have killed herself inside of ten seconds."

"Not many freelance assassins could afford all that," Dirisha said, "nor would they need to bother. Damn."

As she left the medical center, Dirisha was worried. Not being able to break into the assassin's mind gave her almost

as much information as if they had been able to do so. A
Confed agent meant trouble; Rajeem Carlos had become an
official target. The next time, they might field a better agent.
Protecting a client meant more than stopping a series of
attempts. You could win a hundred times, and if you failed
on the next, the game was over. Unless the Antag Union
was looking for a martyr, it was time to take Rajeem to a
low-profile status—invisible, if possible. Something had
changed in the Confed's assessment of her client, and he
was in danger, without a doubt.

And, if she kept protecting Rajeem, she would find herself in direct confrontation with the Confed. Such an act
would be treason, only one among all the other treasons the
Confed named to protect itself. Was she willing to do that?
Was it time to walk? Maybe to find Geneva and head for
the outplanets while the Galactic Confederation went nova?

It was something to think about.

Port said, "There was a call for you. From Renault.
Somebody named Sleel. Must have been important, it was
direkconnek White video."

Dirisha checked to make sure Rajeem was all right, then
went to her external com. If Sleel was willing to spend his
stads on that kind of connection, she could do the same.
She initiated the code.

The image was augmented color—even White hadn't
come up with subspace color transmission, so it was up to
the computer to enhance the color codes sent with the picture—and Sleel looked slightly unreal.

"Hello, Sleel."

He looked nervous. "Dirisha. Pen told me to contact you.
I'm calling all the matadors. Troubles being born."

Dirisha didn't speak, but waited.

Sleel continued. "In the last two weeks, nineteen of our
clients have been attacked. Seventeen assassination attempts

were successfully prevented without serious client or matador injury; one was stopped, but the matador went final chill, with the assassin; one got through. Implosion device, on Greaves. We lost Penderson and Malori."

Dirisha winced. Penderson had been a short, bearded man who was always making jokes; Malori a pale-skinned woman who tended to cry when upset. Shit.

"Does that count the attack on my client?"

"Affirmative. Pen thinks we've got a conspiracy. All our people are protecting anti-Confed sympathizers. Pen thinks the Confed is out to make us look bad."

"Sounds as if they blew it."

"So far," Sleel said. "But Pen doesn't think it's over. They're getting worried, Dirisha. We've had inquiries from local politicos, even those on our payroll. They're checking everything from our building codes to our financial records. We've had people all over the place, poking around."

Dirisha considered that for a moment. Then, "Is Massey still training?"

"Massey? Sure. Why?"

"Nothing important, just curious." If Pen allowed the Confed spy to stay at the school, he must have his reasons. His thinking made a bonsai look like a straight-edge laser. "So what's the scat?"

"Pen wants everybody to know things are heating up. The Confed is going to make some kind of drastic move. Pen thinks everybody should bury their clients in a hole somewhere. The assassins will likely try again."

Dirisha agreed with that. Sleel's message only made it that much more urgent. "Anything else?"

"That's enough, isn't it? If anything else comes up, I'll get back to you. Discom, Dirisha."

"So long, Sleel."

Dirisha stared at the blank air. Now what? At the very least, she had to get Rajeem somewhere safer than he was.

The Confed was powerful, but it wasn't omnipotent. There were places to hide from it.

She had to find one of those places and put Rajeem and his family in it, and fast.

"Impossible," Rajeem said. "I can't serve any purpose hidden under a rock somewhere like some pale grub."

Dirisha looked at Beel, whose face wore a worried expression. The three of them were in the main room of their house—both Beel and Rajeem had insisted the place was now hers, too—but nobody was sitting on the comfortable form-chairs. Rajeem stood facing Dirisha, three meters away, his hands on his hips; Beel twisted at her belt, forming the third point of an unequal triangle.

"Rajeem—" Beel began.

"No! I won't slither off to hide!"

"You're being stupid!" Dirisha said, angry.

He looked surprised at her outburst.

"What you want here is not the important thing, is it? I thought you were dedicated to the fall of the Confed."

"Of course I am—"

"That's not how I see it, Rajeem. You ought to be thinking of the day after tomorrow, not right now. If you're dead, a lot of hopes go with you. When the Confed falls, you need to be around to help pick up the pieces. You can be one of the movers, one of the people who point us in the right direction, afterward."

"I intend to be—"

"No, you don't, not if you won't run when you need to run! I can't protect you against the full weight of the Confederation dinosaur if it falls on you. I'm good, but I'm not a god. Even Khadaji knew when to shoot and when to footprint."

"Dirisha, I—"

"You like the center stage, Rajeem, I can see that. No

dishonor there. But what *you* want isn't as important as what you represent right now. If somebody shoots, you duck, anything else is stupid! And selfish."

He turned away from Dirisha, looking at Beel.

"She's right, Rajeem. You like the game, but you have to look a few moves ahead. If you get taken out before the final round, it'll all be a waste."

Rajeem turned to stare at the wall. He took a deep breath, blew it out harshly, and shivered. He turned back to look at the two women. "I guess you're right. I'm sorry. I was thinking of myself, my ego, how it would look.

"What do you want me to do?"

Dirisha nodded. "I know a place where nobody will ask or care who you are, as long as you pay your expenses."

Leaving one world for another was supposed to be a strict procedure, insofar as identification was concerned. In theory, it was impossible for a person to travel by Bender under a false identity. As in many things, the theory was a far hop from actual practice. Dirisha, Beel, Rajeem and the children left the planet Wu, the system Haradali and travelled nearly eighty light years distant, to the Ndama System, to the world for which Dirisha had been named. And they did so in disguise and with new names, by a route which would be difficult, if not impossible to trace. To a place Dirisha hoped she'd never see again: home.

She was prepared to see change in Sawa Mji, after fifteen T.S. years, but she was surprised in that.

The place looked almost exactly the same. Oh, there were a few new buildings; some of the old ones had been color rebonded or altered slightly, but for the most part, Flat Town seemed little different than when she'd left it.

As the boxcar glided down, Dirisha felt a tightness in her gut. She hated this place, had always hated it, and she

could remember almost no good times to stack against the
bad. But it was the perfect setting for a man like Rajeem
Carlos to hide. Spacers passed through, but only losers came
to stay. The dregs settled in Flat Town, and turned even
more sour as they aged. The Confed was inclined to let the
place rot and die on its own—the military outpost was a
token, no more, and only incompetent soldiers wound up
there. Even if Rajeem stood up and announced who he was,
the local drugged Lojtnant-in-Charge would have trouble
understanding, or know what to do about it. It was a dank
pit, her birthplace, and perfect for this one thing.

Although she felt little for her relatives, were they still
living, Dirisha knew she had to see if they still lived there.
They might recognize her, and they might be curious; therefore, it would be good tactics to survey them.

Even as the boxcar bounced to a rubbery landing, Dirisha
had enough self-knowledge to know her rationalization was
just that. She was curious, and despite herself, she cared.
Her mother and sister and brother were products of the
society into which they had been born; Dirisha knew just
how hard it was to escape their fate. She was well-off now;
maybe she could help, somehow. If it wasn't too late.

Port and Starboard had arrived before them, also incog-
nito, and they were waiting when the boxcar unloaded.
Dirisha felt the wave of heat wash over her as she stepped
into the afternoon, and the stink that she'd grown too used
to to notice as a child hit her nostrils almost like a physical
blow. Chang, how could people stand it?

Port and Starboard had arranged quarters, ostensibly for
a wealthy mining engineer, his sister and her children.
Dirisha and the other two guards would pretend to be nothing
else, looking out for their patron because he was forced to
wait in this scumpit to close a lucrative business deal. The
background story was well-fleshed, and local spies would

find confirmation, if any bothered to check.

After they were settled, Dirisha went looking for her family.

It was as if they had never been.

In the run-down brothel, the owner's cur was surly, at first. "Don' know nuthin', bend off, Sister, you're wastin' my—!" He shut up when Dirisha jabbed the barrel of her spetsdöd into his muscular, but quivering belly.

Dirisha knew what language worked here. The madam's cur looked out for her second, himself first. "I'm not some lacy offworlder, Deuce. You can talk or you can squirm on the floor. And if you reach for the panic tab, you get kicked after you fall."

The cur recognized power. "No—nobody named Zuri working here. There used to be a girl, but she's gone. Had a kiddo, but she went, too."

"Where?"

"I dunno—"

"Guess."

He licked dry lips. "Might try Belvo's."

Dirisha turned and started for the door. She took two steps, then spun and fired both spetsdöds, getting off six darts. None of her shots hit the cur, but his face went dough-white. He'd been reaching for a shotpistol, and Dirisha gave him enough time to clear the counter with it before she blasted the weapon out of his hand. He put his hands on his head, fingers interlaced, and she turned away again.

Belvo's was, if it were possible, worse than the crib she'd just left. And it was a waste of time. Her sister, if it had been her, was gone, along with her daughter. Or somebody else's daughter, maybe. Of her mother, there was no trace at all.

On her way back to her quarters, Dirisha felt a depression like none she'd had since leaving this world a decade and

a half before. What had she expected? That she would sweep
in and free her sister from her bondage? Lay a thick wad
of standards into her palm and tell her to go to a place where
she could live like a human instead of a poorly-treated
copulatory work beast? Yeah, that was part of her fairy story,
to be the sister who escaped, and who finally came back.
It was a delusion, she knew. She was bright enough to see
the bitter humor of it, the last vestiges of the girl she had
been wanting to *show* them! It wouldn't have been for
Zawadi, it would have been for herself. Learning to love
didn't cure everything that had haunted her. There were still
ghosts which had to be laid to rest someday. But not today.

There was a surprise waiting for her when Dirisha got
back to her room. A message from Sleel. Starboard said it
sounded urgent.

Dirisha called. Sleel's image came to off-colored life over
her communicator.

"The shit tube has blown," Sleel said. "The school is
closed, and everybody is supposed to head for a hiding
place. Matador training has been declared Treason Against
the Confed, Dirisha. I'm calling from a sub rosa station Pen
set up, halfway around the planet from Simplex-by-the-Sea.
There are arrest files out for all of us, you included."

"Is everybody okay, Sleel?"

"Last I heard. We had six hours warning. Bork and Mayli
stayed to close the Villa down with Pen, but they got clear
before the Confed troopers rolled over the school."

Dirisha felt relieved. Thank all the gods!

"Everybody who hasn't already hit the road running is
likely to be pulled into a Confed net. Most of the people
with clients have taken off." He paused, and his face seemed
to grow red. "It was Massey, Dirisha. He was a fucking
spy! And you knew it, didn't you?"

Dirisha sighed. "I knew it. But so did Pen."

That seemed to stun Sleel. "He did? Then why did he let it happen this way?"

"I don't know, Sleel. Pen has crooked eyes, he sees things I can't."

"Yeah. Shit. Look, Dirisha, I'm leaving, stat. But I've passed the word to everybody that they can use the quintdrop for messages. Pen says the Confed'll take years to run it down, even if they catch somebody who puts 'em on to it. Call if something happens."

Sleel was silent, as though searching for something else to say. A surge of emotion ran through Dirisha as she thought about the school being shut down, about the Confed destroying the only safe home she had ever known. She felt rage, sadness, helplessness, all wrapped in concern for her friends.

Sleel cleared his throat. "Uh, look, Dirisha, I might not—that is, you and I, we might not be able to–to . . ."

"It's all right, Sleel. I understand. You take care of yourself, you hear? You're a good man, Sleel."

"C–c–copy, Dirisha. Luck on your blindside. Discom."

Dirisha turned, to see Rajeem standing behind her. She wanted to jump and run to him, she felt like crying, but she sat without moving. "You heard?"

"Yes. It looks as if the dinosaur is going to thrash around some before it rolls over and dies."

Dirisha stared at nothing. The school was dead, her friends scattered. Pen had to have known it was coming, he always seemed to know everything, how could he have missed it? More, if he did know—and he must have—why did he allow it to happen that way? What was he up to?

"Dirisha?" Beel looked concerned.

Dirisha started to speak, but the com lit with an incoming call. Absently, she flicked the unit back into life. What now?

It was Sleel again. "Sleel? What—?"

"It's Pen, Dirisha! They got Pen!"

"What?! How? Where? Is he all right—?"

"He just walked into the military commander's office and turned himself in!"

Dirisha shook her head violently. "I can't believe that! Why would he do it? Why?"

"It's on a livecast, Dirisha! Somebody must have known, it's on the net, I'm looking at it! I'm going to try and patch the signal into the com's transmitter—hold it—"

Dirisha's screen blanked, then cleared. The holoproj was fuzzy but the enshrouded figure of Pen was centered in the picture. Dirisha sucked in a deep breath. Pen was surrounded by a dozen armed guards, and an officer moved to stand in front of him.

Gods, if Pen wanted to resist, he could take out most of the room, maybe all of them! He was still wearing his spetsdöds! Were they blind, as well as stupid?

The officer reached up toward Pen's hood. Pen stood impassively, his arms by his sides. Dirisha leaned forward.

The officer grabbed at the covering over Pen's face.

Whoever was operating the camera zoomed in, to a tight shot of Pen's face. The officer's hand closed, as he bunched the fabric of Pen's robe in his fist and tugged. The covering came off, and for the first time, Dirisha saw the face of the man who had been her friend and teacher for more than six years. She let her breath go with a yell as she recognized the face under the robe—

The face of Emile Antoon Khadaji!

TWENTY-FOUR ————

"IT CAN'T BE," Rajeem said. "Khadaji's dead, he was killed by Confederation troopers on Greaves."

Dirisha's mind churned. "It's him. I worked for him, I know what he looks like. Damn, why didn't I recognize him before? His voice—he must have used a throat muter—"

"Khadaji. Alive." Rajeem stared at the now-blank communicator. "There are people who worship him as a kind of messiah. He could probably raise an army of five million by waving his hand."

Port came into the room. "I dunno if this is the time," he said, "but a package came for you." He held out a plastic-wrapped bundle to Dirisha.

Dirisha took the bundle. It was the size of a shoe. Mechanically, she began to tear open the covering. Her thoughts ran unfettered through complicated mazes in her mind. Why?

What was Pen—Khadaji—up to? What did it all mean?
What was she going to do now?

The cover came free, to reveal a flat box. Dirisha opened
it.

Inside, was the curved knife she had seen Pen playing
with in his office, just before she'd decided to leave. She
picked up the thing of steel and brass and wood. Light
glittered from the mirror blade. That it was a message,
Dirisha doubted not at all. What was it Pen—no, not Pen,
Khadaji—had said? The knife had taught him a basic lesson?
What was he trying to teach her now? That she should
remember the ultimate purpose of the matadors? Of Khadaji's intent? She stared at the knife. What else? The knife
was a form of fugue, not nearly as subtle or complex as
many of the fugues Khadaji/Pen had spun. *Your turn, Dirisha*, the knife seemed to say.

"Dirisha?" Beel had come into the room, to stand next
to the seated woman.

Dirisha looked up, and it came to her, all in a rush, what
she had to do. "I need to get in touch with Geneva, and the
others."

"Of course, you're concerned—" Rajeem began.

"More than concerned," Dirisha said. "You said Khadaji
could raise an army if he wanted. The first people in line
would be the matadors. Khadaji was more than just a holo
hero at the school, he was *revered*. It was such a basic part
of our training that Khadaji was the acme of what a dedicated
human should be, the matadors will fall all over themselves
trying to figure out a way to help him. It could be suicide."

"But they'll know that Khadaji taught them that, as Pen."

"It won't matter. I *knew* him, knew he was only a skilled
and lucky man, and even so, I have this urge to hop the
next Bender for Renault and break him out. With most of
the students, Khadaji was set up to be father-mother-lover-

best friend. And even if he hadn't been, all of us are loyal to Pen. We owe him. Ah, shit!"

Rajeem dragged one hand through his hair. "Something strange about all this."

Dirisha laughed. "Strange? Hon, you don't know the eighth of it! Pen has wheels within wheels within wheels going, all the time. Nobody has ever been able to figure out what he's up to, not until now."

"You understand it?" Beel asked.

Dirisha stood, still toying with the knife. "I think so, yeah. Khadaji made his run against the Confed on Greaves as part of a long distance plan. He made himself a legend. He built the matador school based on that myth. The Man Who Never Missed. A to-the-bone hero. He indoctrinated a corps of followers, the matadors, and sent us out to spread the word. Now, he's in trouble. What are we to do, but figure out a way to help him?" Dirisha looked at Rajeem and Beel. "You understand what it means? The Confed has been tottering for a long time. Khadaji wants us to give it a push. The matadors have the ears of scores of the richest, most influential beings in the galaxy; people who, in many cases, owe matadors their lives. People who are already leaning away from the Confed yoke. Think about it. It's perfect. No army or navy can be raised to match the Confed military machine with guns. The real power is wielded by those with influence and money, and the matadors influence *them*. It's fucking perfect."

"What do you intend to do? Tell the others they've been duped?"

Dirisha shook her head. "It wouldn't matter. Most of them owe what they are to Khadaji/Pen. He might have used us, but he also taught us a hell of a lot. And we were all selected because we had little use for the Confed in the first place. No. That's not why I want to see them."

"Why, then?"

Dirisha stared at the knife she held, watching her reflection in the cold steel blade. Why? That was the crux of it, wasn't it? Khadaji had taught her, had molded her. She had been a loner, and he had made it possible for her to be part of a team. She hadn't known what love for another was, and he'd given her that, too. There had been, for whatever his reasons, a home, a place to belong. But there was more, another lesson she was supposed to learn. She looked at the knife. It wasn't enough that she had these things, not in Khadaji's estimation. He wanted something more from her. What?

There was an answer for that, she knew. She had to care for more than herself, or a few cherished others. She had to stretch, to open herself to her fellow beings. It was what Khadaji had done. The long view. It was what he demanded of her.

"I've got to see the others and . . . lead them," Dirisha said quietly.

"Lead them?" Rajeem shook his head. "To do what? The Confed has an army of billions!"

Dirisha grinned. "First, we free Khadaji. After that, we'll see. If we have to drop the Confed, we'll do it."

"That's crazy!" Beel said.

"Probably. But it's what we'll do. Or try, anyway."

Toowoomba Educational Complex, Australia, Southern Hemistates, Earth. In the belly of the beast, or more appropriately, the liver: where the poisons were strained out: the headquarters of the Confederation Armed Forces. What better place to hide?

Dirisha sat in the library alcove, waiting. Rajeem would be okay, Port and Starboard could handle anything Flat Town could throw at them. This was more important, at the moment.

She saw the woman enter the building, a dark-skinned, dark-haired housewife, wrapped in a heavy coat, against the evening chill outside, wearing thick mittens.

Dirisha stood, and the woman saw her.

The skin and hair color were different, but there was no mistaking the smile. Dirisha stretched out her arms, and Geneva came into them. They hugged each other tightly. Geneva started to cry, but Dirisha kissed away the tears. "Hey, Brat, no time for that. We've got work to do."

"Ah, Dirisha, I've missed you so!"

"Yeah, well, I noticed you weren't around, too."

"What are we going to do about Pen? I mean, Khadaji?"

"Don't worry, Hon, we'll work something out. Have the others arrived?"

"Yes. Sleel was the last, he's at the cubicle. Mayli and Bork are waiting outside in the flitter."

"Good. Let's go. We've got a lot to talk about."

Arm in arm, the two matadoras walked out into the night. Dirisha wasn't worried, not in the least. The matadors were going into battle.

The Confed didn't have a chance.

STEVE PERRY

THE MAN WHO NEVER MISSED

Khadaji was ruled by the brutal forces of
the Galactic Confederation—until one day he had
a revelation...and walked away from the battlefield.
He was a new man, unknown, with a secret plan that
he shared with no other. Not his mentor.
Not even with the beautiful exotic whom he loved.
Now, no one can understand how the Shamba Freedom
Forces are bringing Confed to its knees.
No one sees them. No one knows who they are...until
Khadaji is ready for them to know.

_____ **The Man Who Never Missed**
by Steve Perry/0-441-51916-4/$2.95

MORE SCIENCE FICTION ADVENTURE!